"I'm as boring as biscuits,"

Allyn said, backing away from him.

"Biscuits only need a little sweetening—a little jam, a little honey—and they become one of my favorite foods." Ian's voice had dropped to an intimate, luring tone.

Allyn took yet another step backward, but there wasn't any space left between her and the stacked luggage. Her heel banged into the bottom piece. Tottering, her arms flailing in a futile attempt to regain her balance, she landed clumsily on her backside, her knees caught over a suitcase, her feet in the air.

"I don't think I've ever seen a woman get so flustered over a man being interested in her." Ian grinned down at her, his legs braced apart, his hands on his hips.

Allyn sighed. "That's me. The queen of aplomb."

Dear Reader,

If you're looking for an extra-special reading experience—something rich and memorable, something deeply emotional, something totally romantic—your search is over! For in your hands you hold one of Silhouette's extremely **Special Editions**.

Dedicated to the proposition that *not* all romances are created equal, Silhouette **Special Edition** aims to deliver the best and the brightest in women's fiction—six books each month by such stellar authors as Nora Roberts, Lynda Trent, Tracy Sinclair and Ginna Gray, along with some dazzling new writers destined to become tomorrow's romance stars.

Pick and choose among titles if you must—we hope you'll soon equate all Silhouette **Special Editions** with consistently gratifying romance reading.

And don't forget the two Silhouette *Classics* at your bookseller's each month—reissues of the most beloved Silhouette **Special Editions** and Silhouette *Intimate Moments* of yesteryear.

Today's bestsellers, tomorrow's *Classics*—that's Silhouette **Special Edition**. We hope you'll stay with us in the months to come, because month after month, we intend to become more special than ever.

From all the authors and editors of Silhouette **Special Edition**,
Warmest wishes,

Leslie Kazanjian
Senior Editor

VICTORIA PADE
Divine Decadence

Silhouette Special Edition

Published by Silhouette Books New York

America's Publisher of Contemporary Romance

SILHOUETTE BOOKS
300 East 42nd St., New York, N.Y. 10017

ISBN: 0-373-09473-6

First Silhouette Books printing August 1988

Printed in the U.S.A.

Books by Victoria Pade

Silhouette Special Edition

Breaking Every Rule #402
Divine Decadence #473

VICTORIA PADE

is the mother of two energetic daughters, Cori and Erin. She laments that she has never traveled beyond Disneyland and instead has spent time plugging away at her computer. She takes breaks from her writing by indulging in her favorite hobby—eating chocolate.

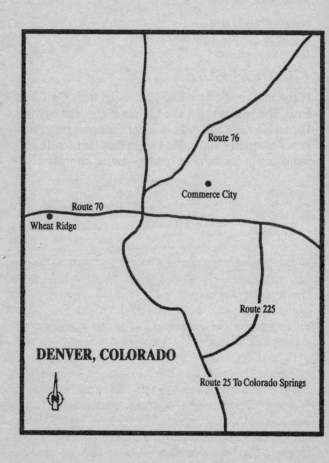

Route 76

Commerce City

Route 70

Wheat Ridge

Route 225

DENVER, COLORADO

Route 25 To Colorado Springs

Chapter One

The streets of downtown Denver were busy with men and women in stuffy business suits as Allyn Danner waited for a group to cross the alley opening onto Seventeenth Street. Her fingers drumming impatiently on the steering wheel, she glanced at the clock on the dashboard of her van. Five minutes to nine. She sighed, cursing under her breath at the young urban professionals who kept coming, ignoring her need to turn.

"Come on, come on," she muttered, taking in the tailored suits and the stylish haircuts. "I know a lowly baker doesn't measure up, but I have to get through anyway." She blared her horn and inched into the turn just as an attractive, executive-type man and his younger, female equivalent stepped off the curb into the alleyway. The two shared a whisper and an intimate laugh.

Love among the cubicles.

The thought made Allyn grimace. She glanced at herself in the rearview mirror to push at a wild strand of her curly red hair, and in that split second she found her blue eyes too big, the close-cropped cap of her hair too short, her cheekbones too prominent, her nose too narrow. She dropped her critical gaze to her clothes. The closest she'd been able to come to dressing for the funeral she was going to be late in attending was a pair of corduroy slacks and a white blouse. A closet full of blue jeans could never compete with the put-together businesswomen that walked the city streets en route to their jobs and office flirting. For just a moment, she felt inadequate.

"No, you'll never be one of them, Danner. Tough luck," she said to herself. And then she hit the horn again—hard.

She'd tried to squeeze in as many of her accounts as possible before the funeral, but, as usual, she had overestimated her own capabilities, and the service was set to start across town in five minutes. Finally taking the right-of-way, she punched the gas and sped into the alley to the delivery entrance of McCauley's restaurant.

Bounding out of the van, Allyn hurried to the vehicle's rear double doors and flung them wide. From the racks that lined both sides of the interior she slid commercial baking sheets laden with small chocolate cream puffs filled with custard. Balancing the sheets, she backed up to McCauley's delivery door and kicked it.

"It's me, Syl. Open up," she shouted. She waited, but nothing happened. "Damn! I'm in a hurry!" she tried, but still there was no answer. "Danner's Decadent Desserts. Let me in!"

Finally sound came from the inside, and the metal door slowly opened.

"It's about time, Sylvia. You know I have a funeral to go to and I'm late already," she said, before realizing that the person who'd opened the door was not the chef's assistant and her friend, Sylvia Pratt, but Carusoe De Vallenzuala, the owner of the chain of semifine restaurants misnamed McCauley's.

"Just what I like: dessert first thing in the morning. What better way to start off this Tuesday, eh, sweet-cakes?"

Allyn cringed inwardly but ignored the demeaning endearment. "Morning, Carusoe. I'm in a rush. Would you let me by?" The sound of his lascivious chuckle was as irritating to Allyn as fingernails scraping against a blackboard. The tall Latin man grinned down at her and winked slyly from beneath thick eyebrows.

"I'd let you do anything at all."

"Great. Then let me in before we end up with soot on these cream puffs."

"Ooo. That gives me ideas. Anytime you want to be my cream puff, just let me know." He finally stepped out into the alley, moving to unload a tray with three tortes on it. Allyn rolled her eyes at his faulty wit and went into the kitchen.

"Hi, Syl," she greeted her friend, who was chopping celery at the long, narrow worktable that ran down the center of one of the cleanest kitchens in any Denver restaurant. Setting the two baking sheets on a side counter, Allyn didn't pause to talk, heading out to the van once more.

"Spread yourself too thin again, haven't you?" Sylvia called after her.

"I do what I have to," Allyn said over her shoulder. By the time she'd returned from three more trips for trays of confections, Carusoe was nowhere in sight and Sylvia was leaning against the worktable holding out a cup of steaming tea.

"I don't suppose you've stopped to eat anything yet today."

Allyn laughed, accepted the cup in one hand, and hugged her short, rotund friend with her free arm. "Wrong. I had a muffin on the way."

"One muffin and you've been up since, what, two this morning?"

"Three. You have flour on your nose."

Sylvia smeared the flour with the back of her hand. Shorter even than Allyn's five feet, Sylvia was very nearly as wide as she was tall—a tribute to her own culinary expertise. The two had been friends since the sixth grade, though with a hairnet covering her pale brown locks and with the excess weight, Sylvia looked years older than their mutual thirty-three.

"They just hired a new man in Howie's office. He's single." The insinuation was implicit.

"No thanks, Sylvia," Allyn said, a warning tone in her voice.

"Howie's worried about you."

"That husband of yours worries about everything." Allyn laughed it off.

"You were related by marriage once. You know Howie, he feels responsible for everybody. He wishes you would at least date someone. We both wish you would at least date someone."

"Let's see, what were Howie and I?" She avoided the subject that had nearly become a litany over the past two years. "In ancient history I was married to his third cousin twice removed. I don't think that makes him responsible for me. Tell him to relax."

"This could be the one. He sounds nice. He's freshly divorced. You don't mind bald men, do you?"

Allyn grimaced, and spoke with careful precision, "I am too busy to be bothered with any man, Sylvia. Period. End of conversation. I have to go."

"You can't go yet. Carusoe said he had some news for you."

"Well, where is he, then? I'm late, already."

"He had a phone call. He'll be right back. I hope you know what you're doing by relying on somebody who calls you 'sweetcakes.'" Sylvia sneered the word.

"Really bad, isn't it?" Allyn agreed with a laugh. "But he's a harmless lech. If listening to his dumb remarks gets me what I want, I'll listen to them all day."

"Is it what you really want, Allyn?" Sylvia sounded dubious and concerned.

"To open my own shop with kitchens big enough to supply ten times what I do now and maybe mail orders, too? The possibility of one day franchising? I think it comes real close, Syl."

"You'd still go home to an empty place every night."

"A blessedly quiet place to do what I want when I want; to eat when I please and what I please, to do my own thing."

"Alone. It's not good. I just read an article that said people are healthier and live longer when they have someone to share their lives with, someone to love."

"And I just saw some shrink on TV who said single women in their thirties are the most mentally stable, happy sector in America today. Besides, I'm healthy as a horse and determined to be the first centenarian baker on the moon."

"No kidding, Allyn."

"Who's kidding? I'll make space the final frontier in franchising. We'll call it Danner's Lunar Delights. Now where is Carusoe? I should have been in Wheatridge fifteen minutes ago."

As if on cue, the man in question came through the swing door, running one hand through his precisely trimmed dark hair. Though some women no doubt thought him attractive, Allyn found his features too severe, his nose too hooked to be appealing—even setting aside his personality. He swaggered into the room with cockiness to spare.

"Great, you're still here. Come back into the office with me."

Allyn knew the pitfalls in that from experience. "We can talk here. Sylvia knows everything. What news do you have for me?"

He shrugged, accepting defeat gracefully. "No news, really. I'm still talking. We want just the right mix of backers. I have a friend who's looking into an investor he knows who wants to diversify. It takes time, sweet-cakes. Trust me. But you're going to have to give a little, not be so standoffish. If you want to win over those of us with the bucks, it takes a little public relations."

"So long as they're public. Why did I have to wait if there wasn't any news?"

He grinned slowly. "Just wanted you to know I was still thinking about you. How's your evening look? We could have dinner. Talk things over."

"Sorry. You line up the backers and then I'll talk."

Again the shrug as he headed back out the kitchen door. "Hard to get. That's what I like. Tomorrow."

Sylvia shook her head. "I wish you weren't involved with him."

"I'm not involved with him. He's offered to find the financing I can't get on my own, and I've accepted. He has experience—he's done it for himself three times over, hasn't he? I'd be crazy to pass this up."

"If it pans out. What if it's just big talk—a come-on?"

"If it was just a come-on he would have given up by now. Lord knows, he hasn't gotten anywhere. And he won't." Allyn glanced at her watch. "Geez, I'm going to miss most of the service. I'll see you tomorrow morning—same time, same stuff."

"Think about that new guy in Howie's office," Sylvia reminded.

"No! No! No!" Allyn shrieked in frustration as she went through the door.

A late September sun warmed the quiet landscape of Mount Olivet cemetery. The last of the mourners filed away from the grave site to their cars parked at the curb of the narrow lane that weaved through manicured green lawns. The leaves of tall elm trees were just beginning to turn to shades of rust and gold, and a few, caught by a light breeze, fell among the headstones.

On behalf of his widowed sister, Ian Reed thanked yet another person for his condolences and headed to the mortuary limousine in search of Emma's sunglasses.

As he felt between the velvet cushions of the back seat, the squeal of brakes sounded directly alongside the mortuary car. Followed by the clank and grind of gears too hastily forced, the vehicle bucked and stalled on the spot. His attention drawn by the unconventional arrival, Ian looked up to see a black van, the side panel emblazoned with bright red script proclaiming *Danner's Decadent Desserts*.

Inside the van, stuffy in the bright sunlight, Allyn wilted. For a moment she felt overwhelmed. She closed her eyes and rested her forehead on the steering wheel. Sylvia was right, she did spread herself too thin. She had always thought she could do more than she actually could. But the option of doing less was something that had been taken away from her. She straightened and vaulted out of the van.

"Bloody piece of junk!" She slammed the door so hard the van rocked. "For two cents I'd run you off a cliff. Don't you have any consideration?" she berated the hapless vehicle. One boot-clad foot struck out at the fender, again and again, as if that would rectify the situation. "If you were a horse I'd shoot you," she railed, releasing her pent-up frustration. "Irresponsible, unreliable, undependable. You have to be male. There's no other excuse. Dynamite up your exhaust pipes—that's what you deserve." Boom, boom, boom—she beat a fist against the hood.

Ian had backed out of the limousine and come up behind the hot-tempered redhead as, still mumbling words of rage, she bent to find the release, and then flung open the hood. It bounced hard and boomeranged back. Ian lunged to catch it before it slammed down on the back of her head as she leaned over the engine.

"Careful! Careful!" he chided.

The woman raised deep cerulean blue eyes to pierce him. "Did you say something?" she demanded with more ice than the entire Rocky Mountain range had seen in ten years.

For a moment Ian only stared at her.

"Well?" she demanded again, even more impatiently, "did you say something? What do you want?"

He smiled—a lazy, disarming smile. "I said to be careful. You nearly got the hood to this heap in the back of your head."

"Heap is right." Allyn's glance went slowly, disdainfully up the length of his lean, six-foot frame, bypassed his face and trailed his arm to where he still held the hood at bay. "Saved by the white knight," she grumbled ungraciously and went back to unscrewing the wing nut that held the air filter so she could get to the carburetor.

Allyn watched the strange man's smile turn into a grin, as if her anger amused him. "Would you like me to take a look?" he asked.

"I don't know who you are, but I don't need your help. Thanks anyway."

"I'm Emma Graham's brother."

That stopped her for a minute, and took the bite out of her tone. "Oh," she said noncommittally and continued with her engine work. "Well, since she only has one brother—to the best of my knowledge—and he's some sort of merger maker, I know you're not a mechanic."

"Not by trade, but I still might be able to help."

Trying to control her temper because of who he was, she said tightly, "I know what I'm doing."

Not releasing his hold on the hood, Emma's brother nodded back over his shoulder at the sign on the side of the van. "Are you Allyn Danner?"

"Last time I looked," she muttered as she worked.

"You're . . . ah . . . quite a surprise."

"Yeah, that's me, full-of-surprises Danner. I don't know what you're talking about."

"I thought I had heard all about you. My sister and her girls think the sun rises and sets with you. Sweet, quiet, thoughtful, warm, loving, generous, gentle, sensitive to a fault, always willing to take over anything to help out, lending them support through Mike's illness. I expected some sort of fairy godmother."

"Or Lassie," she said, without looking up. "Emma and the girls have been vulnerable; that makes even the smallest thing seem like a big deal. I assure you I am no sort of fairy godmother at all. If I was, you can bet I'd turn this pumpkin into a glass coach."

"I wish you'd let me help you with it."

Allyn turned just her head up to him, frowning. "You don't really expect me to believe you know anything about tricky carburetors, do you? Emma talked about you, too, you know. Jetting around the world in private planes, chauffeured around in limousines. I suppose, just for kicks, your driver pulled off the road once and let you give him a hand."

It was disconcerting to have her snideness laughed at.

"As a matter of fact, I'm a very good mechanic. As a kid I rebuilt entire engines. And in a real pinch, I can even change a tire."

"I can't afford the cleaning bill on that suit you're wearing." She went back to work.

"Italian silk spun by the hands of ninety-year-old vestal virgins. Wear it once and toss it out—a law of Vesta. Does that make you feel better?"

"Finished!" she announced triumphantly. "And that makes me feel much better." Allyn replaced the air filter and screwed the wing nut tightly in place. Then she straightened, ignoring the charm of his humor. She reached to close the hood. "Excuse me. I'm late."

"Too late. The service is over. But Emma and the kids are waiting for the interment. Park in front of the limo and I'll walk you to the grave site. They've been asking for you." With his free hand, he took hold of her shoulder and moved her a step away from the van before he slammed the hood back into place.

Allyn jerked away from his touch and ground out peevishly, "I'll make it on my own."

He shrugged, "Have it your way, then."

Allyn climbed back into the van and started it on the second try. Once more it clanked and groaned going into gear, then she backed it up against the curb—*behind* the mortuary car.

All efficiency, she took a rag from beneath the seat and wiped her hands. Chafing inside at the fact that she was inappropriately dressed, she unrolled the cuffs of her white shirt and buttoned them at her wrists. Then she tucked the tails more securely into the waistband of her gray corduroy slacks and yanked up on the high collar that stood sentry on either side of her sharply angled jawbone. Reaching for the door handle, she glanced up and stopped.

Standing only a few feet away, Emma's brother stood watching her. For a moment Allyn stared back. Emma had been right: he was an astonishingly handsome man. Hair the color of sable, square features, a nose that could only be called patrician, a deep cleft in the center of his chin, coal-black eyes beneath a strong brow. He was dashing—the kind of man, the thought came unbidden, that made most of the young executive types downtown look like little boys just playing at being grown-up, dignified men.

Allyn very nearly sneered. Women would throw themselves at him, and she'd bet he caught more than his fair share of them.

Lord, but she was thankful to be immune.

She averted her glance and left the van, passing him as if she didn't see him.

A blanket of flowers was being taken from the casket as Allyn came up to Emma Graham and her twelve-year-old twin daughters. She had only to say their names for all three to come into her outstretched arms.

"He died loving you all more than anything in the world," Allyn said through the choke of her own emotions, her voice soft and compassionate, in sharp contrast to the tone she'd used to berate her van and Emma's brother only moments before. "That love is something to hold on to. Now go on home. You don't need to stay and watch this."

Emma wiped her eyes beneath the black veil of her hat. "Ian said the same thing, but I have to make sure Mike is finally put to rest," she wailed on the wave of new sobs.

"I'll stay," Allyn insisted firmly.

Emma sniffled. "Maybe that's best for the girls. Are you sure you don't mind?"

"I don't mind. It's easier for me than it would be for you. Go on."

Reluctantly Emma and her daughters stepped out of Allyn's embrace, and Ian took his sister's arm. Over her head he spoke to Allyn, "I'm glad you have more influence than I. Just stay until I put them in the car and then I'll come back and do this," he offered.

Allyn turned away from him, speaking to the space in front of her in the same harsh tone in which she had addressed him before. "I said I would do it and I will," she decreed stubbornly, as if his thoughtfulness had offended her.

Ian frowned, but led the way from the grave site without another word.

Allyn stood off at a short distance to watch the coffin lowered into the ground. A shiver ran up her spine and chilled her even in the warmth of the early-autumn day. She clasped her left shoulder with her right hand, holding on as tightly as if she needed to steady herself, her left arm stiff as a board at her side, her hand in a white-knuckled fist.

"She loved you, my friend," Allyn whispered. "She'll miss you. It'll be hard for her, but she'll be all right. Death is a clean ending that leaves the heart with only one wound to heal. One wound. One scar. She wouldn't believe it right now, but there are harder ways for a woman to lose a man she loves; ways that batter a heart until it seems it will never be the same again."

For a moment, memories washed into her thoughts and tightness swelled in her chest as if something heavy sat there. And then she left the grave site, the memories and the hard feelings behind.

An hour later Allyn turned her van up the long drive to Emma's three-story, Tudor-style house. Cars were parked all along the cobbled path that circled a marble fountain in front of the large, imposing dwelling. Outside, all was quiet, serene. The only sounds were the water falling from a cherub's ewer high above the round basin of the fountain and the gentle rustling of the early-autumn breeze through leaves growing brittle. Allyn drove around the house to the four-car garage in back, above which she lived. A push of a button on the remote control clipped to her visor opened one of the heavy wooden garage doors, and she pulled in, thinking of the Graham's generosity.

Eighteen months ago, at the lowest point in Allyn's life, she had met Emma Graham. Just beginning to test her wings in the dessert business, Allyn had placed a classified ad in both the *Denver Post* and the *Rocky Mountain News*, offering to cater any sort of gathering with her concoctions. Emma had been the first person to call, sample the delights of years of baking experiments and hire her. When the older woman had realized that Allyn was living with Sylvia and Howie, baking out of their small apartment oven, she had offered Allyn the use of the living space above the garage. Her rent was cheap, Mike had taken his boat out of the fourth stall in the garage so that she could park the van there and load it more easily, and the entire Graham family had welcomed her as if she belonged. To Allyn, the Grahams' kindness would always stand as proof that for every door that closed, another opened.

She crossed the yard, rounded the enclosed swimming pool and the tennis courts and stepped onto the tiled patio. Two people she had never seen before sat talking on the surrounding knee-high brick wall that supported an ornate wrought-iron railing and tall, old-fashioned streetlights. Four sets of double French doors allowed entrance into the back of the house, but Allyn went in through the single screen door to the kitchen.

Greeted by the loud snort of the Grahams' housekeeper blowing her nose, Allyn crossed to the gray-haired woman and put an arm around her. "How are you doing, Ruby?"

Sniffles answered first, but then her soggy eyes raised to Allyn and she smiled, her overly powdered face creasing with more lines than a street map. "Bless his soul" was all she said.

"Need help?"

"No, no. Miz Graham's been asking for you. You go on in to her. My granddaughter came in with me today to lend a hand."

Allyn gave her a squeeze and passed through the swing door that connected with the dining room.

In search of Emma, Allyn passed through room after elegant room where the Grahams' family, friends and business associates gathered in small, solemn groups. When she spotted Emma she was pleased to see even a wan smile on the other woman's face.

"Allyn!" Emma called, holding out her hand. A tall thin woman with shoulder-length brown hair and nearly perfect features, Emma was sedately stylish. There was an air of sophistication about her, an innate elegance; yet she was so accepting of other people that Allyn never felt the slightest bit self-conscious around her. Taking Allyn's elbow, Emma pulled her in close to her side. "Was it all right?" she whispered, tears coming once more to her dark eyes.

"Yes," Allyn answered simply.

For a moment Emma fought the tears. Then, looking up, she called, "Ian? May I see you for a minute?" Her grip on Allyn's elbow tightened. "Don't you go anywhere! He doesn't bite."

No, but the sight of him did something strange to Allyn's body temperature. He moved with a smooth, easy grace that made her feel uncomfortably warm.

"Ian," Emma began. "This is our Allyn—Allyn Danner. Allyn, my brother Ian."

For the second time that morning, he smiled down at her in that lazy way he had. His black eyes devoured her, holding her own eyes in the warmest of traps. Then he laughed softly, intimately, and raised Allyn's temperature another ten degrees. "We've met. In a way." He extended his hand for her to shake.

Too forcefully, Allyn thrust out her own right hand, overcompensating for the fact that she would rather pet a snake than touch him. Somehow she knew the feel of his skin, even in something as impersonal as a handshake, was going to do just what it did to her—send a shiver up her spine. A pretty face, that was all he was. Just a pretty face. She swallowed. And a body that some treacherous part of her brain kept undressing as it wondered on its own if what looked like well-honed muscle beneath his expensive Italian suit really was. And a voice that was so smooth and gentle and calming that it wrapped around her and drew her in. Lord, where had these thoughts and feelings come from?

"How have you met?" Emma asked.

"She was nasty to me when I tried to help her with her stalled car at the cemetery," Ian teased.

Now Allyn's face reflected the rise in her body temperature by flushing. Indignation, she told herself, not embarrassment. She confided in an aside to Emma, "He's a sexist, did you know that? He didn't think I knew what I was doing under the hood."

"Now, who said that?" he laughed. "I only offered to help before you killed yourself." Then to his sister he said, "Is she always so hostile?"

"Hostile? Allyn? Never. Except maybe a little when that horrible old van of hers acts up and frustrates her timetable. You won't believe the schedule she keeps."

"He won't?" Allyn blurted out in surprise.

"Ian is here to advise in the merger between two Denver banks. He's going to stay and help you watch the house while the girls and I go back East."

Allyn's mouth went dry and something akin to panic streaked up her spine. She hadn't been attracted to a man in two years. And she liked it that way. But here, standing before her, was a man who had cut through that barrier as smoothly as a hot knife through butter. There was something too warm and inviting and kind in his eyes. And too much that looked like appreciation for her in the curve of his lips. Just when Allyn was convinced that she was invulnerable, seriously unwelcome feelings were coming alive in her.

"Oh, well, we probably won't even see each other. With your brother and Ruby both here to take care of things around the house, they won't need me underfoot."

"Ruby won't be here. She told me this morning that the doctor has ordered her to retire. It's her high blood pressure. Ian doesn't know the first thing about what goes on around here. He'll need your guidance."

"He doesn't look helpless to me," Allyn muttered under her breath.

It was Ian's voice that answered, softly, sincerely. "He would like your company, though."

She could feel her heart pounding, and she didn't like it. But this was Emma's brother. Any more overt rudeness would be unforgivable. The only option was to pacify them both until Emma and the girls left in the morning and then avoid him like the plague. "Sure. Right. Well," she stammered wondering how a brief acquaintance could so unnerve her. "I better see how the brownies are holding up. And then, Emma, I'm afraid I'm going to have to make my afternoon deliveries."

Emma reached to hug her friend. "You work too hard. Are you sure you can fit in taking us to the airport tomorrow?"

"If I don't, you'll have to rent a moving van for all that luggage. I'll be back from my morning deliveries in plenty of time." With a spare glance at Ian Reed, Allyn lied, "Nice meeting you."

He extended his hand again. This time Allyn hesitated before taking it. But in the end there was no choice. Big and warm, his hand closed around hers in a way more intimate than the simple formality required, enveloping her, squeezing tighter and holding for a longer time than was proper or comfortable for Allyn.

As if he had read her thoughts about avoiding him, he said, "And we *will* be seeing each other. A lot of each other. I owe you a great deal for all you've done for Emma at a time when I couldn't be here for her." Then the quirk of his eyebrow seemed to warn of his intentions: "And I've always been fascinated by paradoxical women."

Paradoxical? What did he mean by that? Allyn pulled her hand out of his and plunged it into her pocket, opting for ignoring him again. "Take care, Emma. If you need anything tonight, let me know."

Then she escaped—too rapidly to remember to check the brownie supply on her way out.

Chapter Two

When the alarm went off at three the following morning, Allyn was already awake. From her narrow twin bed pushed into a corner of the open-loft apartment atop the Grahams' garage, she stared into the darkness. She had been jolted out of sleep half an hour earlier by a nightmare. But it was something far different from her dream that had kept her from returning to sleep. It was oddly persistent thoughts of Ian Reed. And the rebirth of a feeling she had felt sure she was safe from—being vulnerable to the attraction of a man.

It left her drenched in a cold sweat.

Allyn honestly viewed love and any intimate relationship, any commitment to a man, as a part of life she had experienced and was done with. Like adolescence. Something that by choice—sane, rational, unemotional choice—she would never do again.

Yet, as she lay in her bed, that sane, rational, un-emotional choice seemed suddenly to be in question.

After so long a time, how could the memory of lying in love in a man's arms late at night be vivid enough to make her squirm? But there it was. A trick of the mind. Memories of old sensations arousing a longing. A longing for Ian Reed. For a total stranger.

Determination served her as it had in the past two years, and she squashed the thoughts soundly. Her feet hit the floor with a hard thud, and she flipped the light on, grabbed up her clothes and plunged into her work.

The first order of business was to turn on one conventional and two commercial ovens to preheat. Then Allyn flung open the doors to the three refrigerators that lined one wall and removed mixing bowls filled with the doughs she had prepared the night before. Cake pans and cookie sheets waited on a long worktable that stood in the center of the appliances, taking up most of the remaining space. She began to transfer the various doughs to the corresponding pans as energetically and efficiently as if it were midday instead of midnight.

The recipes were her own, developed from years of experimentation. Cooking had never been her long suit, but she and chocolate had a special rapport. Triple chocolate cookies—chocolate dough with chocolate chips and white chocolate chunks in them—were her specialty and the biggest seller of her cookie repertoire. Following close behind was an extremely thin, crunchy-on-the-outside/chewy-on-the-inside, dark chocolate wafer. She made a version of the standard chocolate chip, hers filled with coconut and just a hint of cinnamon. On Carusoe's advice she had begun to offer her first nonchocolate cookies, using the same dough but replacing chocolate chips with spices and pecans or raisins or orange peel and amaretto.

Tortes were her least favorite concoction to make, so they were what she started with. They consumed more of her time than anything else, but they sold well, mainly because of the rich fudge filling that separated each of seven layers and frosted the outside.

Allyn slid the sheet cakes into the conventional oven, the cookies into the commercial, and turned to the remaining dough. Her personal favorites were the chocolate muffins, rich with walnuts and coconut. Brownies followed, thin and dense. She left some plain and topped the rest with a number of different delicacies— German chocolate frosting, meringue drizzled with stripes of chocolate syrup, caramel and pecans, truffle crunch, cream cheese, or peanut butter.

When all three ovens were filled and the second batches ready and waiting to go in, she set water on the stove for tea. While the kettle heated, she removed three kinds of mousse from molds—one a delicate, light chocolate, another the standard dark and the third, a triple-layered delight of dark, milk and white chocolates.

The piercing whistle of the kettle called, and Allyn poured herself a cup of tea to take with her into the walk-in closet that served as a storeroom for her supplies. Gauging the three different kinds of cocoa stocked there in fifty-pound bags, she made a note to reorder one of the two Dutch processed brands. The white chocolate chunks were getting lower than she liked, too. Imported and sent through the mail, white chocolate would not be sent between May and October. She had already placed an order to ensure its arrival at the soonest possible time. Wondering how much longer that would be, she left the closet to check the date.

Sipping her spearmint tea, Allyn peered over the edge of the Styrofoam cup at the calendar beside the black desk phone on the island countertop that divided the living room from the kitchen.

September twentieth.

The cup stayed against her slackened lips, the steam swirling up into her eyes, the tea in her mouth forgotten.

His birthday. Their anniversary. The announcement. All on September twentieth.

Her grip tightened around the cup, crushing it, and hot tea spilled over her hand, bringing her thoughts back to the present.

"Dammit!" she shouted, dropping the cup and shaking her scalded hand. She hurried to the sink to run it under cold water. "Good move, Al, you jerk. You're really on top of things today. Losing sleep over a strange man and burning yourself over Keith O'Neal. Get your act together, why don't you?"

Just then, the timer went off. Gently drying her hand, she grabbed two well-worn hot pads and went to remove the cookie sheets. Counting one-thousand-one, one-thousand-two, for the thirty-second cooling time before she removed the cookies to the wire rack, she ignored her burned hand and prepared to make the frosting for the tortes. Out came more bowls, butter and powdered sugar; in went three more sheets of cookies, and then Allyn poured herself another cup of tea.

She took a careful sip, and on their own, her eyes wandered back to the calendar. September twentieth. She raised her cup in toast.

"I'd wish you a happy birthday, Keith, but you don't have it coming. You cost me more than you'll ever know. Good riddance."

And then she cleared her thoughts of all but business and picked up her pace in order to keep to her schedule.

Ian Reed stood with one foot propped on the brick wall that edged the patio of his sister's home. Across the yard he watched lights come on in the windows of the garage apartment. Though the curtains were pulled, he could see the shadow of Allyn Danner's movements. Quick and spare, even at the ungodly hour of three in the morning.

In his mind, Ian had a clear picture of her—a picture he liked. She couldn't be more than five feet tall. Thin and lithe, she was long-limbed for her small stature. On any other woman that short-cropped cap of red curls would look boyish, but on Allyn Danner it only accented the delicate, extremely feminine features of a startlingly lovely face. Dark cerulean blue eyes; prominent, high cheekbones; flawless skin; a thin nose, lips just full enough. She was beautiful, but in a totally unique way.

In the silence of the night, muted and barely audible, he heard "Dammit!" sound from inside the garage apartment.

Ian smiled into the darkness and chuckled slightly.

She was full of fire. He liked that. There weren't too many bona fide spitfires in his cultured, sophisticated circles. Or much of the kind of energy she seemed to possess in such abundance. There was something invigorating about that kind of unrestrained energy level. She really was quite a surprise. After Emma's letters about Ms. Allyn Danner, Ian had expected some calm, sedate paragon of virtue. The real thing was so very much more interesting.

And yet, he realized, she possessed elements of the paragon of virtue, too. Her instant transformation at the cemetery from firebrand to caring soul had been surprising—almost as surprising as the fact that she felt and showed Emma and the girls the unrestrained love and concern usually reserved for very close family.

A *curious* woman.

Her affection for his sister and nieces touched Ian.

"Coffee?" Emma's voice interrupted his musings as she stepped from the house behind him. Dressed as Ian was, in a bathrobe, Emma's shoulder-length brown hair was hooked behind her ears and her ordinarily perfectly made-up face was puffy and blotched from crying. She came up beside him and handed him a bone-china cup and saucer that matched the ones she held.

"Couldn't sleep?" Ian asked softly, compassionately.

"The house is too full of Mike. What about you?"

"I'm still on European time. My body thinks it's ten in the morning."

"So you came out to watch Allyn?" she nodded in the direction of the garage.

"I just came out here. What is she doing up at this hour?"

"Baking."

"Baking? Ah, I see. Danner's Decadent Desserts. She must be driven to get up at this time of day to work." He paused and when Emma offered no comment he asked, "Is she?"

"Is she?"

"Driven. To the exclusion of more pleasant pursuits."

"Interested?"

"Mmm." Ian laughed lightly and took a drink of his coffee. "You know me too well, Emmy Louise."

"She's driven. And it's definitely to the exclusion of more pleasant pursuits."

"Now, that is a shame."

Emma's coffee cup stopped halfway to her mouth. "You're one to talk. Who's more work-obsessed than you are?"

Ian laughed. "Maybe that's how I know what a shame it is."

Emma watched him with open curiosity. "I thought you had done your share of wild-oat sowing before you settled down to be Mr. Merger Maker. I remember when you were so impulsive, so free-spirited, that poor Daddy was afraid you'd end up a derelict. Of course, graduating from Harvard disabused him of that concern, but for a while there..."

"Impulsive and free-spirited," Ian repeated as if it reminded him of something long forgotten. "That sounds pretty appealing right now."

"Does it?" Emma asked, sisterly concern and curiosity plainly in her voice.

Ian sighed into the night air. "Lord, but I could use some relief from boardrooms, hotel rooms, merger tables, negotiations...."

"A vacation, in other words. Or is this something more?" He shrugged as he took a drink of his coffee. "I'm just feeling restless. Mike getting sick.... I guess the death of someone close, someone near your own age, does that to you. It makes you begin to question what you're doing, think about all you aren't. Not that

I don't love my job or my life—even if it does get a little lonelier these days than it used to. You're probably right. What I need is a temporary change of pace." For a moment he stared at Allyn's shadow moving behind the curtains. Then he purposely changed the subject. "Your Ms. Danner is not what you led me to expect."

"Of course she is. Do you think I'd lie?" She feigned offense.

"I think you left some things out. Some very interesting things—like that temper of hers. She's quite an enigma. I'd like to know just what it is that makes her tick."

"You aren't thinking of Allyn as your change of pace, are you?" Emma sounded alarmed.

"She is different. Moving in moneyed circles makes you lose touch with her kind of drive and ambition. For some strange reason, just seeing it in her connects me with a younger part of myself—maybe a fresher, less jaded part." He laughed at his own romanticism. "Somehow she feels like liberation from my stuffy life."

Emma sobered. "Go easy, Ian."

He faced her, his expression questioning. "That sounded very protective and mother-hennish of you. Did I grow horns since the last time I saw you?"

It was Emma's turn to watch the garage apartment as she spoke. "She likes to appear tough as nails. And in many ways she is. She's one of the strongest people I've ever met. But underneath...well...underneath she's almost too soft, too sensitive. And she's so man-shy. I owe her more than you know. Thanks would never be enough. I can't see her hurt." She looked him squarely in the eye. "Not even by you."

Ian clasped the back of his sister's neck, squeezing gently as he leaned in and playfully reassured her, "I have never consciously hurt a woman in my life. I'm not likely to start now. Or is she some sort of walking wound that no one can even approach without doing harm?"

"It isn't that. It's just—"

"Come on, tell me her secrets," he cajoled.

Emma's smile was sad. "I don't know them. She's open and giving and extremely private all at once."

"An enigma."

"She's good people, Ian. And she's had a hard time of it."

"I'm good people, too, wouldn't you say?" He smiled down at his sister for a moment and then raised his eyes back to the garage apartment. "And two good people together might just be great."

"For a little while," she added. "And then you'll be off halfway around the world, and Allyn will be left behind."

"Slow down, big sister." He laughed. "I'm just talking about getting to know the lady. Don't go making mountains where there aren't even molehills."

"But you *are* determined to get to know her." Emma's words were more statement than question as Ian continued to stare raptly at the garage apartment.

"I'd say that was the next reasonable step."

"Then I repeat, go easy."

He hooked his arm around her shoulders. "As easy as if she was made of china."

It was utter chaos at ten that morning when Allyn backed the van up to the front door of the Grahams' house. Both Ann and Elizabeth were overexcited, leaving them alternately arguing about who would get the window seat on the plane and crying over leaving their big, unruly Airedale dog, Brit. Emma was frantically trying to make sure everything was packed, the house left in order, and Ian left with more instructions than he would ever need. And Ian was trying to organize the bags and assure Emma everything would be all right.

"Allyn! Allyn!" The twins ran up to her as she came out of the van.

Identical, they shared thin blond hair inherited from their father and wore it shoulder-length and feathered at the sides. But the rest of their features were immature replicas of their mother's. Gangly and awkward some of the time, the rest of the time they worked at being very grown-up.

"Pick a number between one and ten. Whichever of us is closer gets the window seat."

Allyn smiled, put an arm around each of their bony shoulders and closed her eyes, familiar with their decision-making game. "Mmm..." she mused in mock solemnity. "Okay. Got one. Call it."

"Five!" shouted Ann.

"Eight!" rejoined Elizabeth.

"Elizabeth gets it. The number was seven. But the aisle seat is good, too, Annie. That way you get to see when the food is coming."

"Yeah," taunted the wiry twelve-year-old, just as Emma's voice sounded loudly from inside the house.

"Girls, get that dog to stop barking! Those squirrels are teasing her again and all I need is Bud calling the animal control complaining. Get her in here."

The girls began shrieking for the dog as they chased after her, and Allyn rounded the van to open up the back.

"You made it," Emma said from the doorway, relief apparent in her voice.

Allyn climbed the steps and gave her a hug. "I told you I would."

"And I believed you," Emma said without conviction.

Allyn laughed. "You did not. You were worried that my van would break down again and you'd miss getting those two little toads back to their Boston boarding school."

"I never can fool you." Emma smiled wearily. "I'll call Ian to load our bags. We can go as soon as I do some last-minute checking."

"Never mind Ian. I can load this stuff," Allyn said too quickly.

Emma leaned close to her ear and pronounced confidentially, "There are a few details men are good for, you know. They're great with heavy things."

"So that's all I am to you—a beast of burden." Ian came up from behind in time to eavesdrop.

His deep baritone was like thick, warm honey. How could the mere sound of a voice be as soothing as sinking deep down into a tub of hot water? It was as if it washed over every nerve ending, tranquilizing, comforting, renewing. No wonder he was such a successful negotiator. His voice alone probably lulled the parties involved, making them pliable to his wishes. Allyn turned to the stack of maroon leather luggage, stepping around the two trunks that held the twins' belongings, to hoist a two-suiter.

"I'll do that." He was at her side in two steps, forcefully taking the suitcase from her.

"I can manage," Allyn insisted, irritation edging her voice.

"Let him do it, Allyn, you'll hurt yourself," Emma called as she headed into the house, leaving them alone.

Ian set the bag back on the driveway. "It'll work out better if I load the trunks first, slide them up toward the front so we can sit on them and then put in the rest."

Allyn's throat clenched. "So *we* can sit on them?"

Ian looked down into her face, knowing she was trying to avoid him and amused by her discomfort. "I have to see my sister and my nieces off, don't I?"

"Sure," she responded curtly, wishing she wasn't so aware of him. Of everything about him.

He wore a pair of blue jeans that hugged his muscular legs and tight derriere as if they'd been tailored expressly for him. And he looked as natural in them as he had in the expensive Italian suit the previous day. His V-shaped torso bulged beneath a navy blue Henley T-shirt, the short sleeves stretched taut over sharply defined biceps. It was not the physique of a desk jockey, and Allyn unwillingly wondered where he had acquired a body any weight lifter would be proud to own.

Stepping out of the way, she swept the free space between the van's back doors with the wave of an arm. "Have at it, then. I'll see if Emma needs any help inside."

"I didn't say I couldn't use you. You can hand me the smaller bags," Ian said, quick to stall her retreat as he hoisted the first trunk into the van. "Besides, Emma wants to be alone inside for a while. Even though she's just spending a little time back East to recuperate with friends, she feels as if she's deserting Mike or his memory—or something I don't really understand. Anyway, she needs to sort of say goodbye."

That left Allyn with no escape. So instead she counted the bags while Ian lifted the second trunk into the van. Fifteen suitcases. And no doubt the closets upstairs were still full, Allyn marveled with just a little envy, in an effort to think of anything but the man putting those muscles to work only a few feet away. Then she studied the cloudless, brilliant blue sky as if it threatened imminent rain.

"Scouting for pigeons, or are you going to help?" he teased.

Her head snapped toward him. He was watching her, assessing her standard workaday garb—canary-yellow sweatshirt with the sleeves pushed up, aged blue jeans with a patch on the right knee and the left back pocket missing and black sneakers. An appreciative smile curved his lips. Smooth. The man was smooth. But she didn't for a second believe he found her attractive.

She swung a cosmetic case his way, not meaning for it to hit him in the stomach quite as hard as it did. Ian doubled partway over, catching it and his breath with a woof.

"I'm sorry!" She grabbed for the cosmetic case, chagrined. "I didn't... It was an accident."

He straightened, keeping the small piece of luggage and himself out of her reach. For a moment he stared at her, his black eyes boring into her from beneath a beetled brow. "You know, in the past twenty-four hours I've been trying to figure out what exactly it was that I did to make you dislike me. Would you mind enlightening me?"

Allyn felt the heat rise up her neck to her hairline. "Nothing... I... I don't dislike you... It was an accident."

"Accident, my—" Ian stopped himself and took a deep breath. "Look, I'm purposely giving off signals that say I'd like to get to know you better. Does that infuriate you for some reason?"

Allyn took a step backward. "No," she lied softly, embarrassed and very nearly panicked. "I'm sorry, I honestly didn't mean to slug you with that cosmetic case. It really was an accident."

Still he studied her. "Man-shy," he remembered aloud. "Emma said you were man-shy. Is that what it is? You're just leery of men in general?"

Her eyes flashed blue fire. "Emma said that?"

Ian looked to the sky for guidance. "Don't get mad at her now, too. What a temper you have. She only said it kindly, protectively, because she knew I was interested and she didn't want me to bulldoze you. She's told me a lot about you in her letters. She and the girls nearly worship you, and I'm deeply grateful for all you've done to help get them through Mike's illness and death. Top it off with the fact that you are an extremely attractive woman and quite a paradox, and what I'm left with is a perfectly healthy interest in you. Is that so bad?"

The worst. But what could she say? She had already been nastier than anyone had a right to be, and to the brother of a woman she cared for and to whom she owed a great deal. "It isn't that it's bad—" she chose her words carefully "—but I'm one of the dullest people in the world, so your interest is wasted."

His frown eased into a quiet smile. "I'll take the risk."

"No, you really shouldn't," she said—too quickly and much too earnestly.

"I think I have to."

"No, no, there's no reason. Take my advice and ignore me. I'm as boring as biscuits." She shied back another step.

"Biscuits only need a little sweetening—a little jam, a little honey—and they become one of my favorite foods." His voice had dropped to an intimate, luring tone.

Allyn took yet another step backward, but there wasn't any space left between her and the stacked luggage. Her heel banged into the bottom piece, costing her own balance and that of the pyramid of baggage. Tottering, her arms flailing in a futile attempt to regain herself, Allyn landed clumsily on her backside, her knees caught over a suitcase, her feet in the air.

When she looked up it was to see Ian Reed standing directly above her, his legs braced apart, his hands on his hips, grinning down at her.

"I don't think I've ever seen a woman get so flustered over a man being interested in her."

"That's me. The queen of aplomb," she said snidely, pulling her legs from the suitcase so she could get back up.

Before she managed it, Ian grabbed her hand, yanked, and Allyn found herself standing with her nose nearly touching his chest.

He towered above her, a broad-shouldered expanse of pure male sensuality. He smelled like clean country air.

She sidestepped him in a hurry.

"Just cut this come-on, all right?" she said angrily, though there wasn't much force in her breathless voice. "Channel your interest in some other direction; it's not reciprocated. And you can load the luggage yourself. I'm going to help the girls catch the dog."

The sound of his confident laughter followed her as Allyn beat a hasty retreat, refusing to look back.

There was a last flurry of noise and commotion as the girls said goodbye to Ruby and the dog, then argued over which twin the dog liked better and would miss more. Emma suddenly panicked, hyperventilated and announced she couldn't leave after all. But in the end Allyn and Ian managed to get them all into the van where the three turned silent and sad, then wept most of the way to the airport. Schizophrenic emotions that matched what suddenly seemed like a schizophrenic life. Allyn understood it.

It was like emotional stomach flu. The pain came from nowhere—like nausea—and overwhelmed until it had spent itself. Then calmness settled in—an island of respite—and with it came the feeling that you could make it, that you would be all right. But the cycle always brought the pain back again until time wore it out.

Allyn maneuvered the van through the congestion of Stapleton Airport, remembering all too well the roller-coaster emotions of grief—for any loss.

The flight to Boston was early. There were more tears and reminders and reassurances as Emma and the girls inched toward the gate. While Ian teased the twins out of their maudlin moods Emma twined her arm with Allyn's.

"I'll call to see how things are going. Look after Ian—he's used to hotel services taking care of him. He may be a lost lamb alone in my house."

"He'll be fine."

"He'll be fine. I'll be fine. We'll all be fine. Will you be?" Emma asked very pointedly, all of a sudden.

"Sure. You know I will."

"He keeps watching you, do you feel it?"

"Who?" Allyn hedged, knowing only too well.

"Don't play dumb with me, Allyn Danner. My brother is who. Isn't it time you gave a little thought to the male population again?"

Allyn's laugh was forced. "That does seem to be the common opinion, but I'm too busy for that stuff. I'll look in and make sure he isn't swallowed up by the garbage disposal while you're away. Just concentrate on taking care of yourself for a while, okay?"

"Fix him that triple chocolate mousse of yours. It's the most seductive thing you make."

"Seductive Chocolate Mousse—I'll have to use that, it's bound to double my sales."

The last call for passengers to board cut off any more comments from Emma. She and the girls spread hasty kisses around and were gone, leaving Allyn alone with Ian Reed.

She forced a smile to her face and an overly bright tone to her voice. "So. Can I drop you somewhere?"

"From a ten-story building?" he teased, seeing through her. "How about having lunch with me?"

"I eat on the run, thanks anyway."

"Bad for the digestion."

"But good for business. Two-thirds of my customers are restaurants that want desserts for their dinner guests. I don't have time to waste eating."

"All right, then I'll go home with you, spend the afternoon making some calls, and you can have dinner with me when you're finished with your deliveries."

Allyn sighed impatiently. "I have a party to cater tonight, and even if I didn't, I spend my evenings mixing doughs and baking."

"I thought you were up this morning at three to do your baking."

"How do you know I was up today at three?"

"Jet lag. I was up at two. I watched."

Allyn found that disconcerting, remembering that he had been so strongly in her thoughts at that same time. But she decided to address a safer subject. "Most of the baking has to be done in the middle of the night to be fresh. But there are a few things that are better done the evening before. Not that it's any of your business. Am I taking you back home or not?"

He searched her eyes, smiling that quiet smile of his. "You're figuring on dumping me at the house and never seeing me again, aren't you? I'll bet you even have a plan for how to avoid me completely and still water the plants."

"A foolproof one," she assured him as she headed down concourse D, away from the terminals.

"Didn't your mother ever tell you that playing hard to get only intrigues men more?"

"I'm not playing." She was also working hard not to look at him.

"I've broken down stronger holdouts than you, Allyn Danner. Dallas, 1985. Thorton Oil was nearly bankrupt—didn't have the funds to pump the wells they had rigged, let alone drill new ones. The Miller family, who owned all the adjacent land, wanted to buy old man Thorton out. But the old geezer was adamant; the land had to be kept in the family. I took his homely daughter to New York. The best plastic surgeon in the country shortened her nose by an inch and used ape cartilage to build her a chin you could almost see. The best dentist pulled a few of her buck teeth and capped the rest. Contact lenses cured her squint, a fat farm whipped her body into shape and a makeup artist and two hair-stylists did the rest. By the time I got her back to Texas she could have passed for Audrey Hepburn.

Within the week I married her off to one of Miller's sons and the whole deal came as a wedding present."

Allyn took a few more steps, digesting his words. Then she stopped dead in her tracks to look him in the eyes. "That's ridiculous. You just made that up."

He grinned so broadly it was infectious. "Every word of it."

A smile began. "Ape cartilage?" Then, to Ian's delight, she laughed. The sound was full, rich and melodious.

"Is that what gave me away?" His dark eyes gleamed down into hers.

It felt good to laugh, and Allyn suddenly realized how infrequently she did it. "Telling tall tales doesn't fit the image of the dignified diplomat," she goaded lightly in response.

"All diplomacy involves a certain amount of the art. It's more politely called tact—knowing when not to tell the whole truth. Now, what's it to be—lunch or dinner?"

She headed down the concourse again. "Neither. I honestly don't have the time." She walked down the escalator, skirting around people who merely stood still on the descending stairs, and hurried out onto the street.

Ian lunged for her, grabbing her by the arm and pulling her to a stop. "Good grief, lady, slow down. I'm trying to make a date with you."

The feel of his hand was electric. Allyn took it as a warning—no different than if she had touched a live wire with her bare hand—and moved out of his grasp. "I don't date," she said firmly, though the animosity was gone from her tone and the words came out sounding more friendly than she wanted.

"You're working so hard at being a tough nut to crack that I almost believe you. Almost." He drew his thumb along the sharp line of her jaw. How could the slightest touch from him do so much to her? Once more she stepped back out of his reach.

He laughed softly and shook his head at her actions. "If you won't have lunch with me, I'll take a taxi from here into Denver and eat alone. But don't think for a minute that this is the last you've seen of me, lady. Seeing your smile and hearing your laughter only make me more determined to get my fill of them both—and of you. Understand that." Winking audaciously, he hailed a cab and was gone, leaving Allyn, stunned, on knees of jelly.

Chapter Three

"Alll-ynn...!"

"Please, God, don't let this damn van die on me now!"

With her Friday-afternoon deliveries complete, Allyn had stopped to visit her sister Chris—her very pregnant sister Chris. And the newest member of the Patterson family had decided to make an appearance three weeks early, without consideration of the fact that its father was in Washington on business.

"Hang on, Chrissy, we're right in the middle of rush-hour traffic. I'll get you there—Lutheran Hospital is only a few more blocks. Breathe or something." Allyn ignored a yellow light, crossing the intersection beneath blazing red only to have to hit the brake to miss a late left-hand turner. The van gurgled and chugged and threatened to stall. "Don't you dare! So help me, I'll blow you up!" As if heeding her warning the old engine caught and held—hardly purring, but running nonetheless.

"Oooo... Al, I'm in trouble! It's not even three minutes between the pains!"

Allyn swerved around another car and pushed the gas pedal to the floor, blaring her horn all the way. "Just be calm, Chrissy," she said in a voice designed to soothe her sister while hiding the fact that there wasn't a relaxed muscle in Allyn's body.

The blond brick chapel of the hospital came into view. Half a block farther Allyn turned into the emergency entrance and screeched to a halt.

"We're here!" she shrieked triumphantly, and then to herself added, "Thank God."

Chris's puffy hand clasped Allyn's arm to keep her from bounding out of the van. "You'll stay with me, won't you, Al?"

Allyn felt the color that tension had put into her cheeks drain away in a flash. "Sure," she said weakly. "Right up to when they take you into the delivery room."

"Then, too!" Chris insisted as another pain tensed her round face and brought beads of perspiration to dampen her pale brown hair into clinging curls.

Allyn lunged out of the van and ran for the emergency-room doors, hoping sisters weren't allowed in delivery rooms.

Spurred into fast action, two orderlies and a nurse followed Allyn's lead back outside. Within minutes Chris, clinging to Allyn's hand like a vise, was lifted onto a gurney. One orderly rushed them into the hospital and into the elevator while the nurse ran alongside, dispatching the second orderly to notify delivery.

"It's coming! Oh, no, it's coming," Chris moaned. "I don't want to have my baby in an elevator! Don't let it be born in the elevator!"

As the doors slid closed the nurse moved to the foot of the table, reassuring Chris as she went, "Just relax. It wouldn't be the first baby to be born between floors. Besides, it could be worse. Two years ago we had a woman deliver on the front lawn."

"I know. That was me, too!"

The elevator doors opened to the second floor and a howling Chris was raced down the corridor to a delivery room where half a dozen nurses readied everything in a frenzy. Still her sister clung to Allyn's hand while Allyn hoped for a last-minute reprieve. But the baby was coming too fast. Instead of being ordered out, she was instructed to stand at the head of the table and support Chris's back when she arched up to push.

"Pant!" the doctor ordered, and Allyn panted a full five times before she realized he had meant the instruction for Chris.

"All right, now just a little push. Help her up, coach."

Coach? It took Allyn a moment to realize the doctor was referring to her, this time. She braced her sister's back.

"That's good. Rest a minute, now. You're doing fine, Chris. How about you, coach? You're looking a little pale. You're not going to faint on me, are you?"

"No, I'm okay," Allyn lied unconvincingly. Her wobbly knees were barely supporting her.

"Two more pushes and we're going to have a baby," the doctor announced in a happy, yet businesslike voice.

A baby.

Bells went off in Allyn's head. Her stomach tightened and lurched; her throat constricted. But again she supported Chris's back.

It took three pushes instead of two, but the tiny infant girl arrived to fill the sterile room with the sound of angry squawls. Chris breathed a sigh of relief when she was assured that the baby was perfect and healthy, then looked up at Allyn, a worried frown drawing together features that Allyn knew bore only a faint resemblance to her own.

"I'm sorry, Al."

Allyn smiled wanly, her reassurance thin. "You're the one who did all the work." But when the words were out, her breath seemed to have gone out with them. Her chest was tight and she couldn't draw more than a pant less shallow than the birth had demanded of her sister. The baby's cries closed in on her. Allyn couldn't stay in that room—no matter how it looked to anyone.

She ran out as if the place were on fire.

With her feet planted firmly apart, Allyn fell against the corridor wall. She closed her eyes and let her head drop back, taking deep breaths. The words from the song "Don't Cry Out Loud" played themselves in her mind as she struggled to keep her feelings inside.

"Childbirth is nothing to be frightened of."

Allyn had been so lost in herself that she hadn't realized the doctor had followed her out of the delivery room until she heard his voice beside her. "Frightened?" she repeated foggily, raising her head to stare into the older man's kind face.

"I figured your reaction was either fear or queasiness, and since there's very little blood in a birth and virtually none that you could have seen, my vote went for fear."

Allyn shook her head in denial, but didn't refer to his assumption. "Is Chris all right? The baby?"

"They're both doing just fine. They'll be taken to a recovery room to get to know each other and have an eye kept on them for a little while. You're welcome to join them. Your sister was concerned about you."

"She's just a worrier," Allyn said, trying to make light of it. "I forgot to eat lunch today and got a little light-headed—that's all."

The doctor watched her, his expression plainly doubtful. "I can recommend a couple of books for you to read to dispel fears of childbirth," he offered.

"I really don't have a fear of childbirth. It isn't that, at all," she said honestly. "But I appreciate your concern."

Allyn pushed off the wall with more vitality than she felt, hoping to prove she was fully recovered and should be left in peace. No such luck.

"Come on then; I'll show you where your sister is."

"I think maybe it's better if I leave her alone with her baby. I'll go and call the family, and see her later." He had no way of knowing the whole family was on their way already.

"She's asking for you. You can make your calls from the phone in the recovery room."

Allyn's stomach knotted, hoping her reticence wasn't reflected in her face as she followed the doctor to a cheery room with striped wallpaper, where Chris sat propped in bed, cuddling her newborn.

"You okay, Al?"

Allyn forced a smile. "You know me—I skipped lunch again and all the excitement left me dizzy."

The doctor took a courtesy glimpse of the baby, congratulated Chris and then left them alone.

Chris patted the mattress beside her. "Come sit down and see her," she invited.

For a split second Allyn hesitated, but then she perched gingerly on the edge of the bed, peering into the swaddled bundle as if she were about to see something hideous. She laughed, albeit a bit forcedly. "Lord, Chrissy, she looks just like Morey."

Chris grinned and chastised. "What a horrible thing to say about a little baby girl—that she looks like her old great-grandfather. Did you expect her to come out with long pigtails and fluttering eyelashes?"

"I didn't expect her to come out with a crew cut."

"Want to hold her?"

Allyn froze. "No. I'll hold her another time. Isn't it the theory that mothers and babies bond in these first few hours or hate each other for the rest of their lives?"

"I don't think it's quite that drastic." But Chris didn't push it.

A nurse poked her head in to see if everything was all right and retreated, leaving Allyn wishing she could have gone with her.

"Dennis should be here any time now. His plane was due to land an hour ago," Allyn said, trying for small talk, looking anywhere in the gay hospital room but at her new niece.

Chris gave no response, letting silence elapse for a moment. Then she said, "I didn't think it would bother you anymore."

"What?" Allyn played dumb.

"The baby," Chris persisted quietly.

"The baby? Bother me? No. I told you, it was just lack of food and excitement; I think she's great."

"I've wondered about it, you know. I've never met anyone who wanted a child as badly as you did. I couldn't believe it was possible to box that up inside yourself and store it away like raggedy old clothes. But you did such a good job of convincing everyone that I wasn't sure."

"What did that doctor do, give you a dose of philosophy medicine on the delivery table? Don't be silly."

"Make a life for yourself, Al, don't let the past—ugly as it is—keep you from having what you really want." Chris's eyes filled as she watched Allyn steadfastly staring off into the distance.

"Hormones, Chris. You're suffering from an overdose of maternal hormones."

"We both know better than that."

Allyn turned then to look her sister straight in the eye, her words strong and sure. "Yes. There was a time in my life when I wanted a baby. But that time is over. Don't worry about me and what you think I'm refusing myself. I am doing what I want to do. A new path, a new direction, yes—but by choice. You want philosophy? I'll give you some. Life is about change and making your own happiness. What I wanted before is not what I want now. Period. I've changed. What I want has changed. What makes me happy has changed. And all for the better."

"Is it?"

Allyn rolled her eyes heavenward and spoke to herself. "New mothers." Then to Chris she said, "It is. I love you for caring. I love your new baby. But not only do I not covet her, I'm glad she isn't mine. Okay?"

"If you say so," her sister said dubiously.

Just then the recovery-room door opened to admit the new father, bearing a dozen yellow rosebuds and an elated expression on a face with full, flushed cheeks.

Allyn stepped out of the way, gratefully freeing the path to his wife and new daughter.

Within five minutes the room was brimming with family from both Chris and Dennis's side. Relieved to finally escape, Allyn discreetly slipped out.

She kept her gaze unswervingly ahead as she walked past the windowed nursery where bathrobed, slippered women stood with their husband, friends and family. Back in the emergency section of the hospital, the desk nurse returned her car keys—left in the ignition in the excitement and used to move her van into a parking place—and informed her where the vehicle could be found.

Outside, darkness had fallen. The air was autumn cool and still. She spotted the van without a problem, unlocked the door, checked the back as a safety precaution and climbed up into the driver's seat. She automatically slid the keys into the ignition but didn't start the engine. Instead, she stared out the windshield, seeing nothing at all. She sound of an ambulance siren barely penetrated. Her head felt light, but lack of food had nothing to do with it. Her shoulders slumped and she let her forehead fall to the steering wheel, where she rocked back and forth, back and forth.

And around her middle she clasped empty arms.

Standing with one loafered foot up on the brick wall that lined the patio, Ian waited for Allyn to come home. Using the den as his office, he had spent the two days since Emma and the girls had left compiling background data for the merger of two Denver banks. But work had not completely occupied him. He had repositioned the desk to face the French doors that opened off the back of the house, allowing himself an unrestricted view of the garage and the apartment above it. More of his attention had been centered on the comings and goings of Allyn Danner than on the financial statements of either bank. His observations had taught him one thing—to catch her, he was going to have to lie in wait—which was exactly what he was doing.

She was a one-woman whirlwind. And the challenge of that made her all the more intriguing. How she had ever managed to fit helping Emma and the girls into her schedule was causing him more and more curiosity, as well as an increase in his gratitude. Beautiful, driven, tempestuous, generous. Allyn Danner was a woman he wanted to get to know—despite her less-than-encouraging response to him so far.

Ian flicked a mosquito from his forearm, bared by shirt-sleeves rolled to his elbows. Clouds blocked the light of the moon. A cooling breeze sent soft sounds through the stillness and reminded him of an evening that past summer in the countryside on the outskirts of London. A lonely night, that. The estate where Ian had gone to spend a weekend retreat from the city had belonged to a business associate.

The house had been big and empty, as Emma's was now. The grounds were beautifully gardened and too quiet, also as Emma's were. And a cool breeze had been his only company. As now.

Somewhere along the way, loneliness seemed to have become a way of life.

Maudlin thoughts.

He really did need a vacation.

Ian sighed and checked his watch. Past nine.

"Come home, Allyn Danner."

As if in answer, the black van pulled around the house and into the driveway, pausing to wait for the wooden garage door to be mechanically raised.

Ian headed across the yard, all maudlin thoughts dispelled. As he came up to the garage the van pulled into the brightly lit interior and the heavy door began its descent. He ducked under in the nick of time to catch Allyn as she climbed from the van with uncharacteristic lethargy.

"I'm here, don't get scared," he warned, startling her all the same.

Allyn spun to face him. She'd been too preoccupied to notice him coming. "I didn't know you were the kind to lurk in shadows and spring on unsuspecting women in the night," she said cuttingly, though there was a weak edge to the blade of her voice.

"I need you," he answered insinuatingly.

Allyn merely stood staring at him, waiting with her hands thrust into the back pockets of her patched jeans.

"I short-circuited something and can't find the breaker box in the dark. Do you know where it is or at least have a flashlight I can borrow to find it on my own?" The excuse was pretty lame, but she didn't seem to notice.

"Helpless men," she murmured instead, hit the button to send the garage door back up and led the way across the yard to the house. Behind her, Ian followed with a broad grin and an appreciative eye for the gentle, natural sway of those back pockets.

The breaker box was in the laundry room off the kitchen. Allyn flipped open the small metal door, found the single circuit breaker that was off and flipped it up into the On position. The stereo blared back to life and lights flooded the family room and kitchen.

"You're a wizard. Now for the reward," Ian said in a low, husky voice.

Allyn turned to find him standing much too close. "Keep it," she said curtly and sidestepped him to head into the kitchen. She never made it. His hand snaked out around her arm and pulled her in close to his side. His head bent to hers, putting his patrician nose in the proximity of her ear, and he spoke in an intimate tone.

"Pizza, pizza, pizza," he said with as much enticement as one might say diamonds, rubies, emeralds. Allyn's stomach growled in response—mortifying her and delighting him to a laugh that sent the warmth of his breath against her cheek. "Now you can't use the excuse that you've already eaten."

"I have work to do," she said instead, but it came out weakly. Allyn didn't want to be alone. The birth of Chris and Dennis's baby had left her at a low ebb. Going up to the garage apartment to spend the evening mixing cookie dough was unappealing.

"Tell me what you like on your pizza—anything but anchovies—and give me the name of the nearest place that delivers. You can use the half hour before it comes to work, stop to eat, and then go back."

"I told you the other day that I don't stop to eat." But she was persisting only out of perversity and to see how far he would go to insist.

His black eyes captured her blue ones and held them. One of his eyebrows arched up as if daring her to challenge his command, all the while seeming to laugh at his own forcefulness. "Tonight you eat with me. Here or at your place, but I won't take no for an answer."

"Since "No" was not going to be the eventual answer anyway, Allyn relented, smiling slightly at his he-man approach. "Pizza Shuttle. Pepperoni, mushroom and black olives, extra cheese and sauce. But know that I'm only doing this for the food, not the company," she lied.

One side of his mouth quirked up confidently. "Sure," was all he answered, relaying in that one word that he didn't believe it for a minute.

Allyn's phone was ringing when she unlocked her apartment door. Checking the time so she knew when to go back across the yard for pizza, she picked up the phone. The buoyant, revitalized feeling that had come from bantering with Ian Reed deserted her at the sound of her sister's voice.

"Are you all right, Al? We got worried when you disappeared."

"I'm fine, Chrissy. Honest. I figured when the fury died down and you realized I was gone you'd know I just went home to work. No big deal."

"You're sure?"

"Positive."

"Everybody but you was anxious to hold the baby," her sister tested.

"Poor little thing's bones must have hurt when they all finished with her, then."

Silence. Chris was still unconvinced. But in the end Allyn's adamant denial that she was upset left her sister no recourse.

"I won't ask you to come visit us because I don't want you to feel that you have to if seeing the baby bothers you. I just wanted to remind you that I'm available if you need to talk or anything, okay?"

"Will you relax, Chris?" Allyn's voice was tight. "This isn't the first baby to be born since . . ."

"I know, and you avoid every one. You didn't come to see Ashley until she was nearly eight months old."

"I'll be there tomorrow, and I'll hold the baby the whole time, just to prove to you I'm okay, how's that?"

"I'll believe it when I see you. Good night, Al, and thanks again."

Allyn replaced the phone and slumped against the wall. There was no way she could walk into that hospital room tomorrow and look at that baby. No way at all. She scrunched her eyes closed and grimaced to herself. She would say the van had broken down again—and then just hope Chris would drop the subject....

Forty-five minutes had passed when Allyn went back across the yard. But her time had not been spent mixing dough; she had preened. And the very fact of it niggled at her like the taunt of an ornery little boy. She had showered, washed her hair, donned an unpatched pair of jeans and a sweater her mother had given her last Christmas that she hadn't yet worn. She hadn't done it for Ian Reed, she told herself. The shower and change of clothes had been necessary to wash away the smell of the hospital. But there was no rationale for the eye shadow she'd dusted across her lids for the first time in two years. And as for the perfume—she wouldn't think about that at all.

"Ah... Pizza on the patio," Allyn greeted as she came upon Ian waiting for her at the picnic table. A single candle illuminated two place settings, wine in Emma's cut-crystal glasses, an enormous pizza and the man's supremely handsome features. She tried to ignore the awakening of some very feminine feelings deep in the pit of her stomach.

"Humor me," he said with a quiet smile as he stood and waited for her to sit on the bench across from him.

"Something about the air out here tonight is reminding me of another time and place, and I'm sort of reliving it the way I would have liked to do it the first time around."

Allyn sat down, pressing her hands tightly together between her knees. "You've lost me."

"It was a lovely place and a lonely time. I like redoing it with company."

"Ah" was all she could think to comment, but he didn't seem to expect anything more as he served the pizza. Allyn used her fork to primly cut her first bite.

"Come on," he goaded gently. "You're among friends—pick it up and eat it." Which was just what he did.

Allyn followed suit, watching him as she did so. He had a subtle confidence that said he was comfortable with himself; that he knew his own strengths and didn't need to prove himself to anyone. She wished she didn't find that so appealing.

"Emma said you're an investment banker. What, exactly, is it that you do?" she asked, to distract her own meandering thoughts.

He held up his wineglass for a toast and waited for her to do the same. "To a new start between us." He touched her glass with his, letting his eyes rest on her for a long moment before drinking. Then he put the glass down and answered her question. "Actually, the title *investment banker* is misleading—it sounds like someone who sits behind a desk in some old marble building and advises people on how to prepare for their retirement. That's not quite it. I work for myself."

He put his pizza crust back in the box and took a second piece. "I'll give you an example of what I do. Even as we sit here, there is a Denver bank—an old, respected establishment that shall remain unnamed for the sake of its stock prices—that has had a run of bad luck. In the past few years they've made a few disastrous loans, taken some heavy losses with the drop in oil prices and the dissolution of several oil companies out of Colorado, lost money in conjunction with the hard times in agriculture...that kind of thing. They're in trouble. But they are also still a valid concern. They have a number of quality assets, a respected name, a good reputation. With that to offer, they're looking to merge. What I do is put them together with the best partner for that merger. I negotiate with both parties, make the offer and the counteroffers, haggle a little on either side and try to make music."

"And travel all over the world doing it."

"There aren't many corners I haven't seen." He nodded with his chin toward her half-eaten slice of pizza. "Have I bored your appetite away?"

He was definitely responsible for the loss of her appetite, but boredom had nothing to do with it. The man was interesting, attractive and nice. Genuinely nice. And she wished fervently that he wasn't. She was drawn to him in a way she had not been drawn to a man since Keith O'Neal in those long-ago and faraway days of high school. But this was no high-school boy. This was a grown man. And she was a grown woman. And these feelings scared the life out of her. Being with him was a mistake. "I've had enough, thanks. I'd better get back to work." *Back to work? You liar, you. You haven't even started working! You spent your time primping like a teenager.*

"Oh, no, you don't." He reached across the picnic table and grabbed her arm to keep her there. "You're not getting away from me this soon. I've been watching you for two days, and I waited for you nearly three hours tonight. The least you can do is finish your wine.''

She didn't want to leave him. To go back to the garage apartment was to go back to thoughts of the day and Chris's baby. But to stay was...dangerous. This man made her insides feel like mush.

''Just long enough to finish my wine,'' she heard herself say. ''And then I have to work.''

Ian's pleasure shone in the planes of his angular face, thrown into golden highlights and deep shadows by the flame of the candle. There was an aura of power about him that Allyn found comforting and disconcerting at the same time.

His grip loosened and his thumb traced the sharp bone that jutted out from the inside of her wrist, the very spot where she had dabbed perfume. Then he let her go and refilled her wineglass.

''You know, you've tortured poor Emma.''

That startled her up straighter to challenge his statement with widened eyes. ''I have not.''

''Of course you have. She can't figure you out—what drives you, what there is in your past that you don't want to talk about....''

''Who says there *is* anything to talk about?'' she said, too defensively.

''Oh, there is, all right,'' he asserted softly, almost to himself. ''It's right under the surface, erupting at the slightest scratch.''

''That's crazy.''

''Is it? I don't think so. Emma's theory is that a nasty divorce badly hurt you.''

Allyn rolled her eyes heavenward, shrugging the notion off. "Divorce is just a parting. Life is full of them in one form or another."

"That sounds amiable enough. So, if it isn't a hideous divorce, what is your deep, dark secret?"

Allyn stood up, taking her utensils and wineglass with her. "Murder, mayhem and madness. But only one day during every seventh leap year when the moon is full, the creeks are dry and the corn is high. You're safe."

He followed her but stopped to lean against the doorjamb as she rinsed off her plate in the darkness of a kitchen lit only by the glow of the candle outside and the muted shine of a cloud-covered moon. Crossing his arms over his chest, he studied her from beneath a quizzical frown. "Tell me about your work, then. I've watched you run your tail off for the past two days."

"I bake," she said simply, finishing her task and drying her hands.

"Very interesting. Tell me more," he commanded with exaggerated fascination.

Allyn couldn't help but smile. Common sense urged her to leave. Something more elemental kept her there. She leaned back against the counter's edge, thrusting her hands into her pockets and staring at the floor instead of at the too-handsome man in the doorway.

"In days of yore I whiled away my time inventing desserts. Then, overnight, I found myself in need of a means of support. Luckily it was at the same time that being a chocoholic was coming into vogue, and I had an entire repertoire of original recipes. I turned myself into a chocolate peddler. At first it was just making the rounds in offices downtown with cookies, muffins and brownies I sold out of a basket. Then, with the encouragement and inside help of a friend who cooks for

McCauley's restaurant, I branched out into full-blown desserts that I now make for about two dozen restaurants around town, juggling the office sales with the deliveries. At the moment I'm working on gaining backers to open a shop with big enough kitchens to produce in bulk." For a moment the spark of her ambition was a light in her eyes. "Who knows how much I can do with more equipment, even with just a little help...." Then she caught her enthusiasm and hid it. "So. There you have it, my life story. Aren't you sorry you asked?"

"A lady with ambition." He pushed away from the doorjamb and came to stand much, much closer. "But what about your personal life?"

She shrugged, hoping it hid the catch in her breath from his sudden nearness. "There's plenty of that. Why, just today I helped deliver my newest niece." Where had that come from?

Ian watched Allyn's response to her own words. Her face tensed, her brows pinched together, the hollow of her throat constricted. And what he saw in that moment when her guard dropped was a bare flash of softness and vulnerability—the things Emma had described. He reached a hand to the back of her neck in a tender caress. His voice was low and quiet. "That's someone else's personal life. What about yours?"

Heat seemed to rush from his hand all the way through her. Allyn felt at once soothed, comforted and alive in a way she had long forgotten. The scent of her own light perfume mingled with his more spicy aftershave and seemed to go to her head. He stepped closer still, his long legs straddling hers where they were stretched out and crossed at the ankles. His thumb worked around and around against the back of her neck as his other hand cupped the side of her face and tilted it just enough to allow his lips to find hers.

At first the kiss didn't register in Allyn's mind as real. It seemed more a dream, and she drifted with it. His mouth was warm and gently insistent, tugging at her lower lip and then her upper. He tasted of wine, and she had the odd thought that she liked it better from his lips than she had from the crystal goblet. He dwarfed her, but in a most unthreatening way, making her feel wrapped in a protective cocoon. Her toes curled within her leather tennis shoes. Her back arched to him all on its own, and for the first time in so, so long, her breasts seemed to tingle with life, awakening yearning sensations between her thighs.

Had kissing always felt this good? she wondered.

And then she remembered.

Her hands came out of her pockets and shoved him away with a vengeance. She glared up at him. "Not interested!" she shouted and spun away.

But Ian's hand shot to her arm, pulling her up short. "Hold on!"

Her eyes flayed him but she looked as much panicked as she did angry. With intense control she said more distinctly, "I am not interested in this."

Ian took heart from the fact that she hadn't phrased it "not interested in you." "I'd apologize for kissing you, but I enjoyed it too much. I will apologize for rushing you. I've always had a strong tendency to bulldoze when there's something I want."

"I have work to do." When she pulled her arm from his grasp he let her go but laid his palm flat against the opposite doorjamb above her head, barring her path.

"Somehow this got off on the wrong track again," he breathed above her. Then, lowering a contrite expression to her, he spoke sincerely. "I want to get to know you, to spend some time with you."

Allyn didn't like realizing she shared the sentiment. "No," she said emphatically and then softened the blow. "I don't have the time for... anything. I work seven days a week, and the six hours a day I don't work, I sleep. No time," she repeated, reminding herself as well as convincing him.

"There's always a way," he persisted, his implacable determination staring down into her eyes. "And I'm going to find it."

"Good luck," she answered snidely. Ducking under his arm she ended the conversation with an abrupt retreat, nearly running across the yard to the safety of her garage apartment and her ovens.

Chapter Four

The next day did not get off to a good start. Half a slice of pizza and a kiss were all it had taken to set off a surge of adrenaline in Allyn that had kept her awake until after one in the morning. Then the domino effect had taken over. She had slept through her alarm, not waking until nearly five, which had delayed her carefully scheduled baking times and caused her to miss her office rounds completely and make her restaurant deliveries late.

Ian Reed was a troublemaker, she thought as she left skid marks turning into the alley behind McCauley's.

Carusoe De Vallenzuala was waiting for her in the kitchen as Allyn hurried in with cake-laden trays balanced in both hands. The frown that pulled his thick black eyebrows into an unbroken line did not bode well for her.

"You're late," he snarled, motioning three busboys to unload the van.

Sylvia could offer only a silent grimace behind his back as Allyn met him without cowering. "I've already taken ten percent off today's bill."

"Make it twelve percent, or you can turn around and take it all out of here."

Allyn bristled and fought the urge to point out that it was the first time it had ever happened. "Fine, Carusoe. Twelve," she said instead, as if patronizing a demanding child.

One of the Latin man's eyebrows arched then. "I'll settle on ten if you'll have dinner with me tonight."

"Sorry." Allyn reminded one of the busboys about the last tray and turned to Sylvia, hoping Carusoe would take the hint. But he wasn't having any of that. His voice came again from behind, cuttingly.

"Isn't Keith O'Neal your ex?"

Allyn stopped cold. It was a moment before she turned back to Carusoe. "He is" was all she said, leveling icy eyes on his taunting leer.

"I thought so. Did the announcement in this morning's paper about his new position throw you off schedule?" he goaded.

"I didn't see this morning's paper."

"He was made controller for Husby Oil. Megabucks, I imagine, don't you? Bet you're sorry you let him go. How does it feel to lose out on a gravy train to work your butt off baking?"

"Fine, Carusoe. It feels just fine," she answered coolly.

"He must be pretty good. The cream always rises to the top."

"So does the scum."

Carusoe gave a nasty, victorious little laugh as he left the kitchen. "Sour grapes."

"Creep," Sylvia said when he had gone.

"Without a doubt," Allyn agreed, picking up a tray of cream puffs to put in the cooler.

"Are you sure you wouldn't rather give another try to gaining financing from the banks? Then you could tell him to take a flying leap."

"If I thought there was a snowball's chance in hell that I could get a loan through a bank do you think I would put up with him? But you know I tried everything humanly possible. No education, no business background, no prior history, no collateral, no way to pay off the loan should the business fail—so no loan. Period. Carusoe-the-creep is my last and only hope. It'll be okay, Syl. I just need to grit my teeth." Allyn hesitated, wishing her curiosity hadn't been aroused. But in the end she had to ask. "So good old Keith made the papers."

Sylvia shook her head disgustedly. "I was hoping you'd be spared that bit of news."

"It doesn't matter. I would have found out sooner or later anyway. Controller of Husby Oil—well, Keith always did say he was destined to be a big shot."

"Have a cup of tea. You'll feel better," Sylvia offered.

A thin laugh came from Allyn. "I feel all right, Syl. It doesn't matter. It shouldn't even come as a surprise. And anyway I have to go. I'm late for everything this morning."

"Well, I don't feel all right," her friend said as Allyn headed out the door. "If everything that goes around comes around, when is Keith O'Neal going to get what he has coming?"

"I guess we have to trust the fates," Allyn said over her shoulder by way of a goodbye.

"Yeah, yeah, yeah," Sylvia called after her. "But I'd rather cut his brake line."

Allyn chuckled as if she found the whole thing amusing, pausing only a brief moment to kick a beer can down the alley before she climbed into the van, jammed it into gear and laid rubber, leaving.

With his feet propped on the desk in the oak-paneled study of his sister's house, Ian stared across the yard to the garage apartment.

Allyn Danner.

Just the thought of her brought a smile to his face. She was a breath of fresh air—and a frigid gust of wind—either way, a refreshing change to Ian. There was something so real about her. And it wasn't only her clean, natural beauty, although that, too, was more appealing to him than the flawless faces he generally encountered, those products of plastic surgeons' scalpels and unlimited accounts at the Chanel makeup counter. But more than appearance, there was Allyn's watchout/I'm-coming-through attitude. Struggle brought out the best or the worst in people, but whatever rose to the forefront in times of hard work and determination was the genuine article. And this genuine article pushed all the right buttons in Ian. Interested, intrigued, appreciative, attracted...

Funny, he thought. He had worked so hard, so long, so intently, to get where he was. He had never been one to grab onto anyone else's star and be pulled along to the top. Yet now he had such an urge to grab onto Allyn's struggle, to feel the excitement of that drive again, the stirring of juices that success had made obsolete.

Renew. Resurge. Refresh. And all with Allyn Danner, beautiful paradox, woman with a goal....

But part of what attracted him—her ambition, her drive—was what made it difficult to get close to her.

No way. Her parting words repeated themselves in his mind.

There was always a way.

Making the impossible possible was Ian's forte. And when it was something he himself wanted, nothing would stop him. What he needed, he decided, was simple application of the creative manipulation that made him good at merging stubborn business minds.

The wheels in his brain were turning. His eyes nearly bored into the walls of the garage apartment. How to be with the woman, get to know her, to feel again the excitement of striving for something with every ounce of energy?

And then a long, slow smile stretched Ian's mouth. He picked up the telephone and dialed.

"Hi, Melanie, it's me," he said when his secretary's voice sounded through the static of a long-distance call to New York. "I need Jon."

A moment later his partner and long-time friend picked up. "I'll take the Jets and six points. How the hell are you?"

Ian laughed. "You can have the Jets, but only four points. I'm fine. How the hell are you?"

Jon Wyatt's tone turned serious, "Funeral go all right?"

"Good as those things get."

"Emma got here. We had dinner last night, but I didn't want to bring the subject up."

A knowing expression crossed Ian's features. "How is she doing?"

"Pretty good. She looks good, anyway."

Ian chuckled slightly at the barely suppressed admiration in his friend's voice. "Your heart's on your sleeve, Jon."

"Don't make me feel like some kind of ghoul, rubbing my hands in glee over your brother-in-law's death. You know I liked Mike as much as you did."

"I also know you were in love with my sister when you introduced them. That hasn't changed."

"Come on, Ian," Jon chastised in a groan.

"I'm pulling for you, pal. Just don't rush her."

"Who, me?" Jon's laugh was as full-barreled as he was. "You know better than that. I didn't get this paunch from fast action."

"Is everything tied up with the Prout acquisition?"

"The files are closed and the bill paid."

"Terrific. I was counting on you being between jobs. The reason I called is to ask a favor."

"Shoot."

"Come to Denver and handle this merger for me."

Jon groaned again. "So much for pulling for me with Emma."

"I know, I know. It's asking a lot with her in New York and your hopes high. But she's just back there for a visit. I give you my word I'll do everything I can to persuade her to come home soon. Think of it this way: there are a lot fewer distractions in Denver than in New York. You would have more of her time and attention here."

"That's pretty damn feeble, Ian. You must want me there in a bad way. Why?"

"If I say I just can't handle this, would you believe it?" he teased.

"Same as I believe the Broncos are going to beat the Jets."

"It's possible."

"You not being able to handle this merger isn't. You needing your old partner to step in, isn't."

"I need some time."

"For?"

"A woman."

"So do I."

"But your woman is less available. Moving slow will serve you better."

"Says you."

"You know I'm right."

"Sure, sure. What's going on, Ian?"

"Nothing. That's what I'm going to try to rectify."

"Vital statistics," he demanded.

"I want to spend some time with her."

Jon laughed. "I don't consider that vital information. Try again."

"She's different."

"Apparently. You've never dropped everything for any other woman. So, how is she different?"

"She thinks she hates me."

"Hmmm. That is different. I'd like to meet a woman with taste."

"Come to Denver and I'll introduce you."

Jon snarled something unintelligible. "I don't want to meet her that badly. Fate has put Emma in my life again, and you want me to leave her so you can salvage a bruised ego? Give me a break."

"Wrong. I want you to consider the fact that I have been in Europe for the past year handling an account *you* accepted and then didn't want to leave the country to deal with because you'd met some woman that could have been my sister's twin. You owe me, pal.''

"So I owe you. You're asking too much.''

Ian paused, sighed, then searched for the right description. "I'm ... attracted ... curious ... interested in this woman. I *like* her,'' he finished in a very low, serious tone. "Besides, I have never, in the entire time we have been in business together, taken a vacation—that makes me long overdue. And I'll give you the Jets and six points if you come.''

There was a moment's silence before Jon gave in. "And do your damnedest to get Emma back to Denver,'' he reminded.

"And do my damnedest to get Emma back to Denver,'' Ian agreed.

"And if she won't, you take over the merger and I come back to New York to be with her.''

Ian sighed and then conceded. "It's a deal.''

"I'll be there as soon as I can.''

Ian set the receiver back into the cradle, his eyes on the garage apartment once more. "Ready or not, Allyn Danner, here I come.''

It was seven o'clock by the time Allyn got home that evening. Though everything had been behind schedule, the remainder of her day had been good ... and too busy for her to think about the news of her ex-husband's latest triumph. But, taking her mail out of the box at the end of the Grahams' driveway and finding the morning newspaper there, too, reminded her.

She climbed the tiled steps to the outside door of her apartment, knowing she should have dropped the newspaper into the trash barrels hidden under the stairs. But she didn't.

The apartment was warm. Setting the unexplored mail and paper on the countertop, she snapped up the shades that covered each of her four windows, slid them all open and wasted another second to straighten the tieback on one of the white ruffled curtains. Fading September sunlight and the warm smell of fresh-cut grass filtered in. For a moment Allyn basked in both, closing her eyes and breathing in deeply.

But that newspaper waited like an appointment for a root canal. If she wasn't going to throw it out, she might as well get it over with.

She had a drink of water first.

Then she took off her shoes and put them in the closet.

"So, if you don't want to read it, don't," she said to herself, and then muttered under her breath as if the comment had come from a second person in the room: "But you know you're going to."

She went back to the counter and began to flip through the mail.

Bills. More bills. A flier for a K mart sale. A real-estate ad. Another bill. A postcard informing her that the white chocolate would be sent in another two weeks. A notice for a you've-already-won-it prize if only she would go to someplace called Cold Springs. Another bill. There was no more mail camouflaging the newspaper.

Allyn let out a derisive, mirthless little chuckle. "If you had any brains, Danner, you wouldn't open it." But of course she opened it anyway. Curiosity killed the cat.

On the front page of the business section was the article Carusoe had referred to that morning. *New Controller Named at Husby Oil.* Allyn read it without picking the paper up, without getting too close. It was a success story that only alluded to a five-figure salary plus profit sharing.

When she had finished the article Allyn sighed as if she had undergone trial by fire and come out unscathed. "How would you like to know that I don't care?" she said to the offending paper. "I know, it comes as a surprise to me, too. But guess what? I *don't* care. Not anymore. Today I got two new accounts. No, you're right, it doesn't even begin to compare. Small potatoes. But they're *my* potatoes. All mine. No one else's credit. That makes me feel good. And you are not going to make me feel bad. Sorry."

She closed the newspaper and victoriously dropped it into the trash just as a knock sounded on the door.

Standing on the landing outside, a large, covered pot propped against his khaki-clad hip, a bottle of wine in his other hand, was Ian Reed. Tall, impeccably groomed, heart-stoppingly handsome and smelling of spaghetti, he smiled so suavely it made Allyn's breath catch.

"Before you ask, I do sometimes eat food that isn't Italian. It's purely coincidental that last night it was pizza and tonight it's pasta. My cooking repertoire, you see, is limited. How about dinner?"

"How about leaving me alone?"

"Not a chance." His grin was winning.

Allyn sighed emphatically. "Will you please listen to me when I tell you I am not interested in this?"

"Dinner?" He played dumb. "You have to eat. Survival of the species."

"You know what I mean—after last night's episode—"

"Episode? Oh, you mean the kiss that made you mad. Felt good to me. Funny things make you mad.

Anyway, what if I promise not to come near you? We can be friends."

The devilish glint in his eyes was something less than reassuring. But the spaghetti smelled delicious. And, like it or not, knowing better or not, the thought of spending time with him was appealing. "Just friends?"

He raised the wine in his right hand. "I swear on a bottle of Burgundy. Besides, if you leave me standing here with this hot pot against my side much longer, I'll be maimed for life. Take pity."

After a moment's hesitation, Allyn stepped out of the way and let him in.

"Grab the bag I left out there, will you? It's fresh-baked bread—not garlic, but don't hold that against me—the vow of friendship came after the purchase of the bread." He crossed the open space to the conventional stove and hastily set the pot on one of the burners. Then he turned, put the wine on the worktable and looked around.

Ian's gaze made a slow, assessing circle. A tan-covered daybed lined one wall, the plain rectangular coffee table in front of it holding only an alarm clock. A single tweed easy chair sat at a right angle to the daybed, facing a small portable television set. The remainder of the open loft was furnished with ovens, refrigerators and a long commercial worktable that was really an extended butcher's block. Not a rug or a carpet or even linoleum covered wooden floors that were not meant to be bare, and not so much as a knick-knack marred the sterility. Hardly an apartment, Ian decided—this was more on the order of a cot in a kitchen—and a bare kitchen to boot.

"My sister should be shot for charging rent on this place."

Allyn closed the door and met him on the other side of the table, setting the bread down to lean on her forearms, her posterior jutting out behind her. "You should have seen it before," she marveled facetiously. "It was a horrible mess of tasteful furniture that took up too much space, thriving plants I had no time to take care of and thick shag carpeting that was a hassle underneath refrigerators and monster ovens. Luckily she let me remodel."

"Nice taste," he teased.

"Practical. My needs are few."

He frowned around the place again. "Obviously." Then from the front pocket of his plum-colored shirt he produced a corkscrew as if it were a magic wand. "Looks like it's a good thing I came prepared." He watched her slow, quiet smile as she slid up straight, unconsciously arching her back just enough so that her small breasts appeared beneath her yellow sweatshirt. He knew she wasn't aware of the lithe sensuality in her movements, but it did crazy things to his insides just the same. "Set the table," he commanded, seizing the wine bottle to distract himself.

Styrofoam cups and paper plates and napkins on the coffee table were the order of the day. After turning on the stove to reheat the spaghetti, Ian brought the wine. "Now, Allyn," he teased, "don't go all out. Nothing fancy. Let's just picnic."

She shrugged, unoffended. "Best I can offer. Everything except what I need to bake with is throwaway. I do, however, own stainless-steel utensils. No plastic forks for this kid."

"You are a strange woman," he judged kindly as he poured the wine, handing her one cup and taking the other for himself.

"It's a simple life I lead."

"Ha! I know better than that. Remember that I've watched."

"I didn't say it was idle—just simple."

"By choice or necessity?"

"Both. I sold nearly all the amenities to buy the ovens and refrigerators and the rest of the equipment I needed."

"Dishes and glasses being considered amenities?"

"Dishes and glasses being what I had to sell." She raised her nose high and looked down it at him in a silly parody. "Think you're too good for disposable dining, Reed?"

"I think *you're* too good for it." He pointed his deeply cleft chin toward the daybed, made up neatly into a couch. "Sit and relax while I give my specialty a stir."

Allyn did just that, enjoying the luxury. She watched him standing at her stove, his back to her. The nape of his neck, she noted, was thickly corded, giving it the appearance of strength beneath the soft waves of his sable-colored hair. Strength and softness. He was a perfect blending of the two as he stood, tall and straight and confident, stirring a pot of spaghetti. Fatally attractive. Broad shoulders pulled his cotton shirt taut, and her gaze followed the narrowing V to where it tucked into his khaki slacks. Lower still went her glance to a tight derriere. A nice derriere. Whose thoughts were wandering past friendship now?

"You were later than usual getting home tonight," he observed, shaking her out of her study of his backside.

"Are you sure you're an investment banker and not a spy?"

"You've found me out. Industrial espionage. The Keebler elves hired me to discover your secret recipes."

That made her laugh, but she still had no intention of revealing that he had been the cause of the insomnia that had thrown her day off. Instead she said, "I landed two more accounts today. Beginning next week, I'll supply twenty-six restaurants with decadent desserts."

He smiled at her over his shoulder, his coal-black eyes glinting with genuine admiration. "Congratulations."

"Thanks." She beamed back at him, feeling good about it herself.

Balancing the long loaf of bread across the top of the pot of spaghetti, Ian brought their feast to the coffee table and set it on the trivet Allyn had put between their place settings. "Can you handle that much more baking?" he asked as he sat on the floor and watched her slide from the daybed to sit across from him.

Allyn shrugged negligently. "I'll work it out. I'm not worried."

"You already keep a killing pace." He served the pasta.

"I like to be busy," she understated. Glancing around the table she realized what they had forgotten. "I'll get a knife to slice the bread."

He waved her down. "We're *breaking* bread here."

Allyn groaned at the pun but laughed in spite of herself. It struck her suddenly that she couldn't remember when she had felt this good. Relaxed. Contented. Happy. Was it due to the new accounts? Or to Ian Reed? Because attributing it to Ian Reed scared her, she convinced herself it was the new accounts.

Allyn's attention was drawn back to him as he held up his glass for a toast. "To new accounts," he said, as if reading her mind. "I, myself, would like to open one with you."

Allyn touched her cup to his. "To new friendships," she reminded him, but unexpectedly her voice came out in a teasing tone, and she felt her face flush as she picked up her fork to dig into her spaghetti.

"Emma made it to New York without incident," Ian offered as they ate.

"Did she call?"

"No, I called my partner, Jon Wyatt. He's an old family friend. He had dinner with her last night."

"Jon Wyatt," she repeated. "I've heard that name before, but I can't place it."

"He introduced Emma and Mike."

"That's it. Emma thinks a lot of him."

"I hope so," Ian said under his breath.

"How is Emma?" Allyn's voice was soft, sad.

"Jon said she seems okay. Holding her own, I guess. How does anyone really know what another person is feeling or going through?"

"They don't." She answered his rhetorical question sharply.

Alerted by the edge in her voice, Ian watched her. "You're right, I suppose they don't," he tested, seeing that something like anger had been raised in her and he was wondering why.

Agitatedly, Allyn left her fork on her plate and drummed her fingers on the table. "Some things in life are so damned senseless. The wrong people die—people who wouldn't hurt anyone in the world—while slime-buckets who consciously choose to hurt others go on about their business—succeed, even. I'll never understand it."

Ian poured her more wine and just let her words come as she absentmindedly took the glass.

"If life was fair or just, then the people who choose to hurt other people would be the ones to get ugly diseases and die. Not men like Mike."

"Do you have a candidate for an ugly disease?" he asked carefully.

Allyn caught herself then, realizing she had said too much. "Doesn't everyone?" She tried to make it all seem lighter than it had been. "Like Hitler, or someone." She stood then and took her dish with her to throw into the trash on top of the newspaper.

Ian followed her, stopping very close beside her. "Like Hitler or someone," he repeated dubiously. "Or maybe like someone you know personally who has hurt you?"

"Me?" she exclaimed as if the thought was outrageous, and then, as if on second thought, she added, "Well, sure, I suppose if pressed I could come up with a better candidate for death than Mike. He was one of a kind. I cared for him. And certainly Emma doesn't deserve to go through this." She suddenly found it very hard to swallow.

Ian reached a hand to her chin, cupping it gently to lift her face to his. "No more than you deserved to go through whatever it was that hurt you. I'd like to know what that was."

Held in the warmth of his hand and eyes, she could only shake her head and whisper, "Nothing."

His lips formed a tender smile, and his voice was nearly as low as hers. "I won't pressure you. But know that I am not one of the people who hurts others consciously. I'm one of the ones who avoids it at all costs."

She believed him. And in a mind that experience had left suspicious, that was saying something. When he pulled her into his arms she went instinctively, suddenly in need of just the feel of another warm human spirit. She reached around the broad hardness of his chest, resting her cheek against the soothing beat of his heart. His long, powerful arms encircled her, one hand holding her head, his thumb tracing a line within the short cap of her hair.

It was solace she needed and found in that embrace. There was no explanation for it. He was, after all, only a stranger. A stranger who didn't even understand what wounds he was soothing. But there in the closeness of his body around hers, in the momentary loan of his own strength, she found a comfort she had not known in a long, long time.

Then she realized it felt too good. And anything that felt too good for too long was too hard to live without. And anything that was too hard to live without made you too dependent on the person who provided it. And that made you too vulnerable and too needy. And Allyn believed in self-reliance and independence.

She pushed away from Ian with an embarrassed laugh. "Just friends, remember?"

Her need to distance herself was obvious. Ian recognized it and didn't push to hang on to the closeness they had found for so short a time. It had come out of pain and sadness, and although he wanted to ease that pain and sadness, he wanted the closeness they shared to be something more than that—something pleasant, uplifting and joyous.

"You're a great pasta chef and I enjoyed the meal, but I have to get to work," was how she politely asked him to leave.

"Want the leftovers?" was how he let her off the hook.

"I think you'd better take them. Emma told me how hopelessly helpless living in hotels has left you. She would never forgive me if I deprived you of your single source of food."

"*How hopelessly helpless living in hotels has left me.* That's pretty good. I'll bet you can rattle off Peter Piper like a pro."

"A talented tongue."

"I'd like to find out."

"Friends, remember?" she repeated yet again, red-faced at her own unintentional allusion.

"I was hoping you'd let me forget it." He put the lid back on his pot and picked it up.

Allyn opened the door for him, standing just to the side for him to leave. Without warning he bent and pecked her lightly on the cheek. "Don't work too hard, love. I'll see you tomorrow."

She closed the door behind him, unnerved by the realization that she did want to see him again, and that tomorrow couldn't come soon enough.

Chapter Five

When Allyn opened her door in answer to the knock at three-thirty the next morning, Ian stood leaning his shoulder against the jamb, a thermos cradled in his arms and his eyes closed. Allyn's gaze went from the top of his damp hair to the crisply new yellow sweatshirt he wore over a button-down-collar white shirt, to jeans and spanking new tennis shoes. She had to laugh.

"What is this?"

Only one eye opened to peer at her as that same side of his mouth quirked up in a weary smile. "Ian Reed reporting for duty, ma'am," he drawled.

"As what?"

"Baker's assistant, delivery assistant—you name it. You're the boss."

"And you're not a baker's assistant or a delivery assistant."

"I am now." His other eye opened beneath a stern frown. "Are you going to keep me standing out here in the middle of the night, or can I come in out of the dew?"

"I think you had better come in, all right, and tell me what you're up to now."

He pushed off the jamb and ambled in. "Ever think of getting a plain old nine-to-fiver?"

"No," she answered emphatically.

He set his thermos on one of the few clear counter spaces. "Cup, please."

Allyn obliged him. "Not a morning person, I take it?" she said wryly.

"Is this morning? Not even if you're a farmer." He held out the cup of steaming coffee he had just poured from his thermos. "Blended especially for me from a mixture of Colombian and Peruvian beans. Guaranteed to open your eyes."

"No, thanks. I drink tea. But I think you had better inject it intravenously, or your eyes may never open." She watched him breathe in the aromatic mists of steam rising from the cup, smile contentedly, take a sip as if it were the nectar of life and then sigh, replete. "Needed that, did you, Reed?" She laughed again. "Now, tell me what you're doing here."

"I did tell you what I'm doing here. I came to work."

"I don't need an investment banker."

"Here's how it is, Ms. Danner." He leveled those coal-black eyes on her, suddenly wide-awake and brooking no rebuttal. "I want to spend some time with you. Don't say it. I know, you're not interested in romance or involvement or anything that has to do with any person whose feet are bigger than yours or whose shirts button on the wrong side. Duly noted. But on whatever terms, I intend to see more of you. As far as I can tell from watching, my only chance for more than an hour at a shot is to go to work with you. So... My partner will be in Denver soon to take over the bank merger, and I—'' he just barely bowed ''—am at your service. All on terms you can understand. Not romance. Not involvement. Work. You get an assistant. I get to spend time with you. A viable compromise and not a bad deal for you.''

''I think I need a chiropractor.''

''You've lost me.''

''For a persistent pain in the neck,'' she said without animosity. ''I can't agree to this,'' she said more seriously.

''I don't know why not.''

''I can't afford to pay for an assistant, for starters.''

''Money, you mean? If you knew how much I make you'd want me to pay you. I'm on vacation—that makes it absolutely forbidden for me to earn income.''

''Look, Reed, this is just crazy. There's no way—''

''Don't say it. In one of your few unguarded moments over pizza the other night you told me you wonder how far you might be able to go, with even a little help. Why not give it a test run? You're on the verge of gaining backing, of expanding; why not get a preview of what you can do with an assistant?''

Now he was talking in terms Allyn understood. ''I don't know about this,'' she said, but she was obviously wavering as her thoughts raced. It would be a good experiment having a full-time assistant. It could give her some indication of how much work could be relegated to someone else, of how many people it would take to handle the increased business she planned to drum up, of the pros and cons of hiring inexperienced—and therefore cheaper—help. If she could train an investment banker to be not only an efficient baker but to handle the delicate cookies and tortes, too, then she could train anyone. And couldn't she also time how long that training would take and judge whether it was worth it?

With all the benefits seemingly for her and no way to refute his logic, Allyn was suspicious. "What's in it for you?"

He smiled, seeing by the play of emotions on her face that she had found a reason to accept him. "You wouldn't understand or begin to believe me if I told you. Let's just say it's a transfusion."

"You're right, that doesn't make sense."

"So just accept it and use me to full advantage."

She thought it over a moment longer. How much influence came from her own attraction to the man? That put a damper on it. Still, on a purely professional basis, it was a tempting offer. There was no other way she would be able to test so many aspects of being more than a one-woman organization for free. And the information she could garner would be so useful . . . maybe even invaluable.

A transfusion? What was that supposed to mean?

Still, her decision seemed to make itself.

"This is no joyride, Reed," she warned. "I don't have time for fooling around."

"So you keep telling me," he said, with full insinuation.

"I mean it. No games. If you slow me down I dump you."

He rolled his eyes to the ceiling and spoke as if to someone he alone could see. "Have you ever met a harder woman? Sheesh!" Then, to Allyn: "When you see how much help I am, I will expect a full, formal apology. There's more here than a pretty face.''

A lot more. That's what was so distracting. But to him she said, ''You've been warned.'' As the words came out of her mouth, the timer rang. Allyn tossed two hot pads at his stomach. ''Okay, assistant, see if you can take those cookie sheets out of the oven without burning yourself. Set them on the racks on the counter, count off thirty seconds and then holler.''

Ian saluted, winked and turned to the wall of ovens. Clumsy with the unaccustomed task, he opened the oven door, reached in with the hot pad and promptly burned his hand.

''Ouch!'' he said in reflex just about the time Allyn came back with five bars of white chocolate.

''Off to a good start, Reed? Run it under cold water.'' She took the hot pads and removed the cookie sheets, counting as she watched him grimace with pain. ''How much help did you say you were going to be?'' she teased.

''Do you provide workmen's comp?''

''Slacker. I know your type—hire on, purposely injure yourself and then reap the benefits.'' She slid the cookies carefully off the pans with a spatula. ''If you think you're going to live, you can unwrap that white chocolate and break it up into pieces. It's scored, room temperature and has no sharp edges. Think you can handle it?''

As he passed—much nearer than space required—he leaned to speak into her ear. ''I hope you're a better baker than comedian.''

''When things are under control you can sample cookies, muffins or brownies for breakfast and judge for yourself.''

They settled into a compatible silence broken only when Allyn gave instructions. Ian really was more hindrance than help, and it wasn't just because he was slow at the few tasks she gave him. Too often her glance slid his way, lingering on his handsome patrician profile or his large, manicured hands leaving flour smears on the pockets that cupped his tight rear end. Her thoughts wandered from what she was doing to remember the feel of his mouth on hers, to want more.

"Do me a favor, will you, boss?" The deep baritone of his voice snapped her attention from the study of the cleft in his chin. "My hands are full of gunk and I need my sleeves rolled up."

"Gunk? That is not gunk. It is brownie dough, and how did you manage to get it all over both hands just by stirring it?"

"Pure talent." He held his arms out to her ministration.

Touching him did interesting things to her nervous system, something like subtle electric shock. It was a feeling she had never experienced before. Just static electricity from the ovens and Denver's dry climate, she told herself, but she knew better. His wrists were broad and masculine, sprinkled with coarse, dark hair. She would have liked it better if he had warts, she decided, trying to focus her concentration on the safer subject of his dime-thin gold Piaget watch circling his left wrist.

"I'd better take this off. I don't think even expensive watches are brownieproof."

"Good idea." He made the clasp accessible by turning the inside of his wrist up to her. Slipping her fingers under the band, Allyn found the soft warmth of his skin even more unnerving. She made quick work of removing the watch and hastily retreated to the other side of the worktable.

"Ready for breakfast?" she said overly cheerfully.

Ian looked at Allyn curiously, wondering if the expensive watch had somehow offended her, but decided not to comment. "Sounds good" was all he said.

They perched side by side on two bar stools at the island counter, he with another cup of his coffee and she with her tea. Ian sampled warm cookies while Allyn watched.

"I think you named your business right. This stuff is definitely decadent."

She laughed, watching him take a warm chocolate muffin. "This isn't the decadent stuff. This is the breakfast stuff."

"You mean it gets better?"

"Richer. Sweeter. More decadent."

"I take it your goal is to put the entire state of Colorado into diabetic shock."

"Just the state? Why stop there? How about the rest of the world?" She laughed. "Actually, it isn't my goal to fatten up America. That," she said imperiously, "is an unfortunate side effect of the product I provide if enjoyed without moderation."

His dark eyes studied her thoughtfully. "What is your goal?"

Allyn shrugged negligently, making light of it. "The same as everyone's. To be able to pay my bills."

Ian glanced at the round wall clock. It was 5:00 a.m. "Try again," he said dubiously, turning back to her. "Any job would pay your bills. You work obsessively."

"Look who's talking. From what Emma says, you aren't exactly a loafer. One of two partners in a multimillion-dollar firm by the time you were twenty-eight? I suppose you managed that in a mere forty hours a week with lots of idle time?''

He grinned.

Her heart took two beats.

''So it takes a workaholic to recognize a workaholic. But no matter what you say, I think there's more driving you than just being able to pay your bills. How many bills can you have, anyway? You don't even subscribe to cable TV.''

''I'm trying for a stock portfolio,'' she hedged facetiously. ''Break time is over. Back to work.''

For a moment he watched her, curious and appreciating the sight of her. Every movement of her compact frame was efficient yet lithe and limber. There was nothing of the frenzied action he would expect in doing the work an entire staff of bakers would be more likely to accomplish. Dressed in blue jeans that had seen better days and a sweatshirt—blue this time—she was no less appealing to him than if she'd been in silk. His arms itched to be around her, his hands to cup that great little behind that peeked out from underneath the too-big sweatshirt, his mouth to taste more than her handiwork with chocolate.

It was Ian's turn to force his thoughts from straying.

''Slave driver,'' he said in answer to her back-to-work order. ''What's next on the agenda?''

''Eternal stirring of truffle fudge filling. Then we build tortes.''

An eternity was just what it seemed as Ian beat the rich concoction of chocolate, heavy cream, butter and cognac in a bowl surrounded by ice water until it was finally the consistency of warm fudge. After watching the mixture turn thick and satiny, he couldn't resist dipping a finger in for a taste. Allyn slapped his hand.

"No fingers in the frosting, Reed. I run a clean place here," she chastised like an affronted bordello madam.

"I'm a clean guy," he defended with a raised eyebrow and a glint that said he hadn't overlooked the unintentionally ribald insinuation.

The real advantage to having Ian's help came at seven when it was time to load the van, cutting by half the number of trips down the stairs to the garage. By seven forty-five, they were in the middle of rush-hour traffic.

Ian relaxed in the passenger seat, one hand holding his right ankle on top of his knee, while the other hand held yet another cup of coffee. "So tell me how the rest of this day goes."

Allyn kept her eyes on the line of cars in front of her rather than chance lingering too long on the pleasure she found in looking at him. "First I deliver at a restaurant downtown called McCauley's because the cream puffs have to be refrigerated. Then I make the rounds at several offices."

"Where some lucky people are just *beginning* their day."

"I beg your pardon." She chanced a glance over at him. "If you are implying that I am unlucky, you are mistaken. Part of what I do is to avoid having to work like that. I'd suffocate and go insane playing office politics."

Ian watched her, seeing that something more was hidden beneath the surface on this particular subject. He responded to her heated tone. "Well, I wear three-piece suits and spend most of my time in one office or another—without suffocating or going insane, or playing office politics. It isn't all bad. There are some advantages."

She teased him in return. "The fact that you wear three-piece suits comes as no surprise. One look at that tailored, button-down shirt you're wearing like a vestment hidden under your just-bought-for-the-occasion sweatshirt is pretty telling."

"Have you ever tried the nine-to-five route?"

"No." It came too quickly and sounded defensive. "I didn't go to college. I wouldn't fit in."

So that was what lurked under the surface. His voice was gentle. "You're right, you wouldn't fit in. But not from any lack of education. You wouldn't fit in because you're unique—one of a kind."

"Museum quality?" she asked derisively. "Something old and dusty that belongs on a shelf? A dinosaur?"

He frowned over at her. "Not at all. A rare work of art to be savored."

The subject made Allyn uncomfortable. She changed it and went back to what had initiated this conversation. "When I run out of offices or goodies—whichever comes first—I go home, grab something to eat, put the finishing touches on the rest of the tortes, fill and glaze more cream puffs, unmold mousses and load up again for the dinner dessert deliveries."

Still he watched her with those penetrating black eyes. But he let her drop the original subject. "And what about tonight? Catering, carting, what?"

"No catering tonight. I only do that occasionally. I spend the evenings cleaning, mixing dough, making mousses, getting everything ready to start all over again at three the next morning. Don't worry. If you can't keep up I'll understand."

"Ha!" he exclaimed in mock outrage as she pulled into the alley behind McCauley's. "Don't bet on it, boss. I'm in for the long haul."

It was Sylvia who opened McCauley's delivery door in answer to Allyn's knock. The sight of Ian following behind, carrying tortes, made her jaw nearly drop to her ample chest.

Allyn leaned close as she passed her friend in the doorway. "Close your mouth, take a breath and blink, Syl. I know he's the best-looking delivery boy you've ever seen, but he'll expect me to give him more than a dollar an hour if you keep that up."

"Very funny," Sylvia retorted without taking her eyes off Ian.

Good-naturedly tormenting her friend, Allyn didn't introduce Ian to Sylvia until the entire van was unloaded. "He's Emma's brother," she explained, when she finally did the honors.

"The big-deal businessman?" Sylvia blurted out.

Allyn wrapped an arm around her red-faced friend and deadpanned to Ian. "She doesn't get out much."

"You have this man delivering cream puffs?" Sylvia whispered loudly to Allyn.

"Worse than that," Ian answered. "She had me making them at four this morning."

Sylvia smiled and talked through her teeth, out of the side of her mouth, "Why didn't you tell me about him?"

"You have to excuse my friend," Allyn explained, all innocence. "She isn't used to my having an assistant."

Recovered, Sylvia got in a jab of her own. "An assistant, my foot. I can't believe she's with a man. I was beginning to think she was allergic."

Ian laughed. "She keeps trying to convince me she is. I had to force myself on her."

Again from the side of her mouth, Sylvia said, "What are you? Crazy? He wouldn't have to force himself on me." Then to Ian, "Maybe you and Allyn would like to come to dinner."

Allyn growled and Ian laughed.

"Subtle as a Mack truck, isn't she? He's a busy man, Sylvia. I'm a busy baker and you're a busy wife, mother and chef, remember?"

"I'd love to bring Allyn to dinner at your place, Sylvia. Just persuade her and name a night."

Before anything more could be said, Carusoe charged into the kitchen, coming up short when he saw Ian. "May I help you?" he asked nastily of the taller man.

"He's with me, Carusoe," Allyn offered in defense.

"Oh?" the Latin man filled the single word with enough acid to be a lemon. "Who is he?"

"A friend."

"A friend," he mimicked nastily. "I didn't think you had any *boy*friends. I thought maybe you were saving yourself for me. Or am I just good enough to do your dirty money work?"

"Come on, Carusoe. You know that isn't true. I appreciate what you're doing for me—though I wish it was going a little faster. Don't make a big deal out of nothing."

Although she spoke confidently and there was not so much as a hint of wheedling in her tone, this was the closest Ian had seen her come to humbling herself. He didn't like it. And he didn't like this arrogant jerk who had caused it. He stepped slightly, protectively, in front of Allyn. "I'm—"

That was as far as he got before Allyn stopped him with a hand on his arm and her voice raised to drown his. "Have you talked to any of the backers you had in mind, Carusoe?"

He gave an insolent little snort and a bare shrug of only one shoulder. "No, I haven't. And if you're bringing someone else into the picture—" he sent a sour sneer Ian's way "—you can count me out. You don't need two of us selling you."

Allyn couldn't see Ian's face, but she felt the angry tautness in the biceps she still had a hold of. Once again she jumped in before he could say or do anything. "No one," she said firmly, "is working on investors but you. Ian is a friend. He has nothing to do with my business."

Carusoe eyed Ian up and down, then said in a huff, "For your sake, sweet cakes, I hope he doesn't have anything to do with anything."

When the other man had stormed back out, Sylvia made amends to Ian. "You'll have to excuse him, he has the hots for Allyn, and I think you've hit a jealous streak. On top of it, things aren't going well around here. Business is down, and we were dropped a star in this month's restaurant reviews. I told him he couldn't cut portions and have it go unnoticed, but he didn't believe me. Now he's paying for it. Sorry."

Embarrassed by her friend's candor Allyn led the way out, speaking to Sylvia over her shoulder. "Hope he isn't biting your head off. See you tomorrow."

Once back in the van, Ian angled into the passenger seat to face her. "I don't know whether to apologize for being there and causing that or to be mad at you for taking it."

With her hand ready to turn the key in the ignition, Allyn stopped and looked over at him. "Neither. Outside of chocolate, what I do is none of Carusoe's business. And Carusoe is none of yours."

"What exactly *is* Carusoe?"

Allyn started the engine and headed through the alley. "He owns McCauley's and three branches of it. I told you I was working on gaining backers. Well, the way I'm working on it is through Carusoe. He's pitching the idea to some of the people he knows."

"And you have confidence in that slime? You know for a fact that he's trustworthy?"

"I've tried everything else, and he's my last chance. Sylvia's worked for him for ten years. He knows what he's doing. If I have to take a little verbal harassment along the way... well, I guess that's like steep interest on a loan." Once more she glanced over at him, the look in her eyes as determined and driven as anything he had ever seen. "I am going to succeed at this. I'll do what I have to do."

"What the hell does that mean?" he nearly shouted, a deep frown beetling his brow.

"Not what it sounded like. It means I'll put up with being called sweet cakes." She nearly spat the words. "It doesn't mean I'll do anything else. Besides, it's not the way it looks. Carusoe is all hot air," she finished, as she pulled into a parking lot for the next leg of the morning's deliveries.

As it did every morning, the flirting tone of the offices she frequented with her basket of goodies grated on Allyn. She had good reason to be irritated by the intimacy generated among people who spent forty hours a week cooped up together, but today was worse than it had been since the first time she had stepped foot on a high-rise floor and experienced for herself what had done such damage to her own life. Today she had Ian Reed at her side, and a new element was added.

He was a striking man—but more, his suave sophistication stood out like a diamond among polished quartz. There wasn't a predatory female who missed the distinction. Sales surpassed anything Allyn had ever done before, but so did the level of her irritation at the coy, friendly banter, aimed now at Ian, that break time brought out.

It wasn't jealousy, she told herself. It was disgust over grown women acting like hormone-raged adolescents. But she was glad when every brownie, cookie and muffin had gone and Denver's downtown was behind them.

Lunch was sandwiches that Ian had made, since Allyn didn't pause for anything formal. While she decorated tortes with bittersweet chocolate leaves and flowers fashioned with a pastry bag, he went back to Emma's house to make phone calls.

By two o'clock they were in the van and on the road again. Deliveries in the afternoon involved less personal contact, speed and efficiency being necessary to reach the widely spaced restaurants Allyn supplied. Between Ian and Allyn, little more than the location and order of the next stops was discussed.

Five o'clock found them finally back home for the day. But just when Ian thought they would take a break and relax, Allyn informed him that while he was free to stop, it was her pattern to finish the preparations for the next day before showering, eating dinner and going to bed.

"You're the boss," he claimed gamely and kept up with her.

Three hours later she finally plunged her hands into her back pockets, arched her spine, let her head fall far back and groaned with a weary stretch. "Done."

Ian lifted his shoulders up and back, then rolled his head around in a circle. "Just when I was hitting my stride," he declared facetiously. "Do you realize you work seventeen-hour days, Ms. Danner?"

"I try not to count." She also tried not to think about how much she disliked the thought of his leaving now that the day was finished. His help had been nice, but his company had been better. *Debonair*. Allyn decided that that was a good word for him. He was witty, charming, funny, confident and easy to spend even long hours with because he never took himself too seriously. It was a deadly combination. Too easy to like. Too easy to get used to having around. Too easy to want never to lose. She held her hand out very formally. "Thanks for today. You have my sincerest, formal apology for doubting your abilities—you really were a help, and I'm getting a good idea of how much I'll be able to take on once I can afford to hire some people."

Ian looked down at her hand and then up into her eyes. "And you really are nuts if you think I did all this just to be dismissed at eight o'clock. Now is when the benefit of my unpaid employment comes. We can shower—separately—don't get that look. Have dinner, a little wine and relax. Or else I contact the labor board."

Not even a trip to the Caribbean sounded better at that moment. She knew she shouldn't. She also knew she couldn't resist. "Only if I provide dinner. You've done it the last two nights, not to mention lunch today."

"As long as you don't feed me chocolate. I think I taste tested enough today to last a month."

Half an hour later they met in the family room of the main house for what Allyn had prepared on Sunday and intended to eat all week—cold fried chicken and potato salad. Ian supplied a bottle of white zinfandel wine and set paper plates on place mats on the oak coffee table in the center of the paneled room.

"I wanted you to feel at home," he explained of the arrangement, but the truth was that he preferred the close, cozy atmosphere of the plush shag carpet and the deep-cushioned sectional sofa to either the kitchen, the formal dining room or the patio.

French doors stood open to a soft breeze with the portent of autumn's coolness that the still warm days lacked. The room was done in colors of clay and sand, lit only by a single bean-pot lamp on an end table.

When they were done eating Allyn sat up on the couch, sinking into the overstuffed cushions to finish her wine. She kicked off her shoes and carefully put her stockinged feet on a clear space on the low, square coffee table.

From his perch on the floor, with his back against the side of the brick hearth, Ian looked up at her, enjoying the way the soft light gilded her short-cropped cap of curls like a halo around her head. One of his knees was bent to prop his arm, and his hand hung loosely gripping his wineglass.

"I love the way you look. Did you know that?" he said quietly.

Allyn let her head fall back to rest against the pillows. She was unaccustomed to wine. As usual, she had eaten very little. And, also as usual, she was bone tired.

Together they left her with no will for denying the compliment she would ordinarily have argued against. Instead she basked in it, let it feed her morale and teased, "No, I didn't know that. Is it important?"

"In the vast spectrum of the universe, no, I don't suppose it is. But I'm enjoying it, anyway."

She smiled and closed her eyes. "Wine and fatigue-hazed vision, no doubt. But thanks all the same." Behind her closed lids she had a picture of him just then. Well-groomed, his square features masculine and perfect, his body big and hard, his movement at once dignified and graceful. She loved the way he looked, too. But she would never say it.

"I wonder if you realize how few women could wear their hair that short and still look feminine, let alone beautiful?"

"It's purely occupational. I can't sell hairy cookies," she explained practically.

"Do you know what I would give to make love to you?" he said so matter-of-factly it sounded philosophical and completely nonthreatening.

"A goat, seven camels and a sack of snuff?" she joked in response, her eyes still closed, her body so relaxed she didn't seem to have a form beneath her freshly donned jeans and navy sweater.

"Maybe even more." He laughed, producing a warm sound from deep in his throat. "I can't be friends with you, Allyn."

"You'd rather be my enemy?" But her teasing response was only a camouflage for what was actually stirring to life inside her. She felt so at ease with him— something she had never again expected to feel with a man. Warmth stole from her toes all the way up her body and left her languorous, her nerve endings alive and waiting on the surface of her skin.

In this odd mood she was undisturbed when he came to sit beside her, pulling her to rest back against his chest, his arm wrapped around her, just below her throat, to grasp her other shoulder. His big body cupped hers, cradling her. Somewhere far back in her mind a voice told her to move, but she ignored it. This was just too nice. Instead she kept her eyes closed, wiggled a little, settled and said, "I understand now. You'd rather be my pillow."

"Better that than your buddy," he whispered, pressing a breath-heated kiss to the top of her head. "Let me in, Allyn Danner, let me in." He kissed her earlobe and then lower, to the curve of her neck into her shoulder.

Awakening within her were feelings long ago put away and forgotten. Nice feelings. Good feelings. Gentle sparks tingled her to life so that when Ian's palm curved against the side of her face to turn her mouth up to his, she didn't resist.

His lips were dry and felt like sunshine warming her soul. Tender and tentative, he drew her upper lip between his, released it and then took the lower one, before letting his mouth cover hers fully. Allyn's lips slackened and parted and let his tongue come in and tease hers playfully, around and around.

He smelled of spicy cologne. His freshly shaven face was cool and had the texture of a nail buffer against her much softer skin. His arms, turning her into his body and encircling her, held her with just the right amount of firm, unyielding pressure and gentleness.

There were no thoughts in her mind. Only sensation ruled and retaught her the joy of losing herself in just that. She filled one hand with the waves of his hair where it grew at the back of his neck, not only the color of sable, but with the texture of it, too. Her other hand was pressed against his chest, hard and strong and powerful.

Ian's mouth trailed kisses down the arched column of her neck to the deep hollow of her throat as he slid her sweater up and found what he had only suspected—that she didn't bother with a bra beneath her oversize sweatshirts and sweaters. Reveling in the silk of her skin, he found his way to her breast.

Livening shocks of electricity chased away the thickness of lava in Allyn's veins. A small, helpless groan found its own way out of her throat. How good it felt to have his hand cupping her, kneading her, gently pinching her hardened nipple.

Feeling his bare skin became an obsession. Hurriedly she pulled up his own lightweight cashmere sweater, baring a chest softly covered with hair. Both her palms drew up the tautness of his rib cage to find honed pectorals and male nibs that responded to her fingers in the same way hers did to his.

Awakened. That was what Allyn's entire body was. Awake and alive with every nerve exposed and shouting with joy to no longer sleep. Wonderful. Exhilarating. Exciting. She could not get enough of the feel of his skin against her own, in the palms of her hands splayed against his broad back.

Their mouths sought and found each other once more, hungry now, and lacking inhibition. His hands cupped her derriere and held her up tight to his own straining flesh; a desire every bit as starved as Allyn's raged in Ian.

And then the doorbell rang.

"Let me in, you old son," Jon Wyatt called cheerily from the front of the house.

Their lips parted guiltily. Ian dropped his head to the top of hers, sighing, then chuckling. "Somehow being interrupted in the middle of necking on the couch seems easier when you're fifteen."

Allyn was just coming to her own senses. "Not when you're fifteen." She managed the words but failed at her attempt to sound as if she were taking what had happened between them lightly.

As he eased her sweater down and back into place he said apologetically, "It's my partner. I have to let him in. I'll be right back."

The moment Ian was gone, Allyn ran. Through the French doors, across the patio, over the tennis courts, around the swimming pool and up the steps to her apartment as fast as she could go.

Only when she was safely behind her closed door did she stop, leaning for forehead against the cold wood. "Oh, my God," she breathed to herself in horror of what she had let happen, at the feelings that had come alive in her and were still driving her to be with him, to make love with him.

When Ian knocked on the outside of the door a scant few minutes later, she jumped away from it as if it had burned her.

"Let me in, Allyn," he demanded in a husky whisper that echoed with the frustration she felt.

"Go away, Reed," she tried, her own voice weak and gravely impassioned.

"Dammit, I won't go away. Open this door."

"Please just go away. I'm tired," she lied feebly.

"Now, Allyn."

Slowly, hesitantly, she opened the door only a few inches, peering out at his chest since she couldn't bear to look at his face, into his eyes. "A dumb mistake. Just let it go," she said in a barely coherent rush.

"It wasn't a dumb mistake, and I will not let it go. I have feelings for you, Allyn. Strong feelings. And I know you have those same feelings about me. Something is so damn right between us. We have to feed it and nurture it and allow it to grow."

"I don't have to," she answered, letting stubbornness hide her panic at the thought.

"You have to, because I'm not going to let you do anything else."

"Go away."

"Tonight I'll go away because it's late and I know you're tired. And I won't see you tomorrow because I have to get Jon set up and introduced to the people I've been dealing with on the merger. But after that, Allyn, I won't go away. I'll do whatever it takes."

She closed the door and locked it as if that would protect her.

"No!" she shouted through it. But there was no answer, no sign he'd heard her before he left—or had taken it seriously if he had.

Whatever it takes.

It didn't take much. Not much at all to weaken two years' worth of resolves and lessons learned from harsh experiences. How could that be? She had thought she was so strong, so unreachable, so impregnable....

Impregnable.

A pain-filled moan erupted into an almost hysterical laugh.

When it came to Ian Reed, she wasn't strong or unreachable or impregnable.

And that knowledge scared Allyn Danner to death.

Chapter Six

Allyn's telephone rang at a quarter to seven the next morning, just as she was about to begin loading the van.

"Hi, it's me." Her sister's voice on the other end was as tentative as if she were calling to reconcile a heated argument and wasn't sure what her reception would be.

"Chris." Allyn's response was less than overjoyed. Reflexively her glance darted around the room in search of an escape before realizing that she had no recourse but to talk. "How are you?" she asked in a rush of words that mingled her real concern for her sister with her own panic.

"We're doing great. Tired, but great. You know how it is with—" Chris caught herself, amending, "Newborns rule the roost. She keeps the whole house up from one in the morning to about four, then sleeps like a log most of the day. But that will get better."

"But you're feeling okay? And the baby... I don't even know what you named her."

"Holly Nicole. I'm feeling almost back to normal, and she's healthy as a horse."

Allyn relaxed a little, leaning her elbows on the counter as she talked. "How is Ashley taking to the invasion of a new sister?"

"Yesterday she tried to feed her marigolds, and last night she nearly clubbed her in the head with an ashtray—I guess that's sisterly love in two-year-old form. But basically she's good with the baby."

"Listen, I'm sorry I haven't been able to get over. I've been swamped. Not only did I pick up two new accounts, but Emma's brother is staying at the main house while she's back East and, well..." Somehow, explaining Ian seemed difficult. But the pause only served to alert her sister's curiosity in the direction Allyn had been floundering for a way to avoid.

"Don't tell me. You've let a man that isn't one of our brothers or an employer into your life?" Excitement and disbelief sounded together in her voice.

It suddenly occurred to Allyn that this was an excuse her sister would not only accept, but accept with relish. In fact, it would please the whole family, distracting them all from the real reason behind her evasion of Chris's new baby.

What harm could it do?

Allyn's mind raced with possibilities. This was a way out. And then, later, she could just tell her family things hadn't worked out on the romance front. It was a means of keeping her distance now and even of getting the whole lot of them off her back for the future by easing their worries that she would forever cloister herself in her work. It seemed perfect.

She cleared her throat, tried to sound just a little giddy with a small, girlish laugh, and admitted sheepishly, "I didn't invite him, but Ian Reed is in my life just the same. Yes." True enough.

"Tell me," her sister demanded.

"There isn't a whole lot to tell. You've heard Emma talk about him—Ian. She really didn't do him justice, though. He's gorgeous, intelligent, has a great sense of humor and seems like a genuinely nice guy."

"Wow! That would be high praise coming from anyone. I can't believe it came from you. I was—we were all—beginning to think you would never have anything to do with another man in your whole life. You don't know how good this makes me feel."

"I'm glad," Allyn said truthfully. "Anyway, he started out just sort of showing up on my doorstep when I came home at night, but now he's called in his partner to handle his business in Denver so we can see more of each other. You know my schedule doesn't have much free time. He actually shows up here at three in the morning to help with the baking and then goes on the deliveries to be with me," she finished with another laugh.

"And he's rich, too, isn't he? This is a catch, Al. Congratulations."

"Don't get carried away, Chrissy. This is just the pursuit stage. It probably won't work into anything. But for now, for a change, I'm kind of enjoying the attention." She downplayed, not wanting to get in too deep.

"You never know..." Her sister's voice trailed off hopefully. "I can't tell you how much easier it is to make this call knowing you are finally letting yourself come back to the living and have hope for the future, too. Now I really can believe that you've put all the past behind you. Dennis and I want you to be Holly's god-mother.''

Heat rushed up Allyn's spine and flushed over her. Before she could speak, Chris went on.

"You're my only sister and you know I wanted you to help baptize Ashley. Of course, I understood, but Holly will be our last baby, so this time it's more important than before."

Allyn closed her eyes and let her head fall all the way back. Was there a way out of this? ''That's really nice, Chris, but are you sure it wouldn't cause problems with Dennis's family? You know how his two sisters fought over the chance to be Ashley's godmother. Maybe it would be better to let the other one help baptize Holly. As much as I'd like it, you know I won't get mad if I don't do it.''

"His sisters pull each other's hair out over every-thing. I don't care about that. I want you."

There was nothing else she could say. Allyn took a deep breath and let it out again in a silent sigh through slackened lips. When she answered her voice was soft, and she hoped her sister would think it was caused by sentiment. "If you're sure about Dennis's sisters, then I'd love to be the baby's godmother."

"It won't bother you?"

"No, not at all." *Oh, what a tangled web we weave....*

"Terrific. I know this is short notice, but you know how mother is about baptism—she's just sure it's tempting the devil to wait any time at all. We've gotten the church for three on Sunday, and then I'm having a picnic afterward. Will you please bring Ian?"

"Oh, I don't know about that." *When first we practice to deceive!*

"I'll call and invite him myself, if you think I should. If the poor man is going so far as working that godawful schedule you keep, you at least owe him an invitation to the social part of your life, don't you? And you know how we'd all love to meet him."

"I'll see, but I'm not promising anything, okay?"

"Sure. Do you want to come to the house before the service or just meet us at the church?"

"The church, I think. That way I'll have plenty of time for my Sunday deliveries."

"At three, then. I'm so glad about everything, Al."

"See you Sunday." Allyn set the phone back on the hook.

At three o'clock on Sunday afternoon she would have to appear before her family, hold that baby and act as if it didn't bother her in the slightest.

"Pull this one off, Danner," she challenged herself. "Neat trick if you can do it."

Ian found Jon Wyatt at the stove when he came down that morning. At five feet eight inches—if he stood very, very straight, Jon was barrel-shaped, though not more than fifteen pounds overweight. His hair was a salt-and-pepper version of Allyn's short-cropped curls, his eyes were a lively blue and his cheeks were chipmunk full.

"French toast," he announced over his shoulder to Ian as his long time friend poured a cup of coffee.

"I like the apron," Ian teased with a nod at the garment that covered Jon's starched white shirt and red tie. His sleeves were rolled up and out of the way, and a spot of egg marred the perfect shine on his black wingtip shoes.

"I thought it suited me. You know pink is good on everybody," he deadpanned. Expertly, Jon slid thick slices of French toast onto two plates and brought them to the table.

Ian sat looking at the garage apartment between the plants on the shelves of the greenhouse window. "I want to get this merger completely turned over to you today," he said without taking his eyes away.

"So you've said three times since I came in last night. That shouldn't be a problem." Jon lavishly buttered his toast and covered it with warm maple syrup, watching his friend surreptitiously. "I haven't seen any stirrings from across the yard."

"She left shortly after seven."

"Eat up before it gets cold," Jon said, taking a bite as Ian reluctantly pivoted to face the table and his breakfast. "So if you were up watching her leave, why didn't you go over and say good-morning?"

"I didn't think it was a good idea. We didn't part on the best of terms last night."

"I'm sorry about that. Emma suggested I stay here. If I'd had any idea I'd be barging in..." Jon cleared his throat. "I've already arranged a room at the Marriot downtown. I'll go there when we're finished tonight."

"You don't have to do that," Ian said halfheartedly.

"It's done. How about your part?"

"My part?"

"Of this deal. Have you talked to Emma about coming home?"

Ian became very interested in his breakfast. "Not yet."

"Reneging on me?"

"You know better than that."

"Good. Go call her before we leave," Jon urged, nodding in the direction of the den as he used his napkin to clean the egg off his shoe.

As Ian waited for the New York operator to ring Emma's hotel he sipped a second cup of coffee. It wasn't that he was reneging on his part of the deal, it was that he didn't have a clear plan on how to lure Emma back here when it had been Ian who had persuaded her to go in the first place.

His sister's hollow-voiced hello on the other end of the line replaced his quandary with concern.

"Are you all right, Em?"

"Ian? Hi. I didn't expect to hear from you. Is something wrong?"

"Does something have to be wrong for me to call? I just wanted to talk to you and see how you're doing. From the sound of your voice, not well."

Emma gave a soggy little laugh. "I'm okay."

"You haven't been able to fool me since you were six, remember?"

"Oh, Ian," she whispered. Then her tone regained some strength. "I'm not sure it was a good idea to get away from home. Maybe I'd be better surrounded by my own things. Life seems so strange these days. I don't know whether it's me or everyone else, but I feel as if I make everybody uncomfortable. Seeing Jon was good—he didn't act any differently—but you went and called him to Denver. I guess I'm just a little crazy, right now."

Even had it not been to his advantage, Ian would have insisted she come home. Only sincere sympathy answered her. "It's a crazy time in your life, love. There's no reason you have to stay there."

"I don't know." She sobbed softly into the phone. "Can you hang on a minute? My nose is dripping."

Ian waited, feeling like a rat for having taken Jon away from her. When she came back on the line his tone was cajoling but firm: "There isn't a reason in the world for you to stay in New York and be miserable. You went to rest and get away from painful memories, but obviously one location is as bad as another for that. I'm here, Jon is here, Allyn is here. Get on the first plane back."

Emma laughed a little, more in control of herself. "How is Allyn? Is she ditching you successfully?"

"She's really something," he answered admiringly.

"I take it you've managed to wear down her defenses?"

"Let's just say I'm working on it. Come home and be my ally."

"I'd probably be more in the way than anything."

"Hey, this is your house."

"That's right, it is, isn't it? See how crazy I am?"

"I'll call and get you a reservation on the next flight back."

"Thanks, little brother, but I can do those things for myself. You're as bad as Mike was about thinking we women needed taking care of. I love you for it. I loved him for it. But I have to get used to doing for myself now."

"Just trying to help." He feigned affrontery, happy that she sounded better. "So, what will it be, Ms. Modern Woman?"

"Lord, I'm so confused I don't even know what day this is."

"Good, Em. Today is Thursday. How well can you take care of yourself if you don't even know what day it is?"

"Don't be funny. I think I'll go back to Boston and spend the weekend with the girls. Then I'll come home."

"You're sure you don't want me to make your plane reservations?"

"Positive. But thanks anyway." She paused for a moment. "How is Allyn? You didn't say."

From beneath a curious frown at his sister's concern, Ian glanced out at the garage apartment for the hundredth time that morning. "She seems fine. Why does it worry you?"

"Oh, I don't really know. In September of last year she kind of fell apart. The only thing Mike and I ever found out was that there was an anniversary of some sort that month. I've been so wrapped up in my own problems, it just occurred to me the other day that here we are, nearly through September again, and I haven't had my head out of my own mire long enough to notice how she was doing."

"If she's upset about something I haven't seen it. But I'll keep a closer eye on her just in case."

Emma laughed slyly. "It won't be too much of a hardship on you, will it?"

"I think I can bear the burden. If you let me know when you're coming in I'll pick you up at the airport."

"Thanks. If I need you, I'll call. Say hello to Jon for me."

"Oh, I will. I will."

Ian hung up, thinking about his sister's comment on his inclination to believe women needed taking care of. She was wrong about that. He didn't believe they needed it. He just liked doing it. It was part of any strong feelings about someone, to want to do for them, to protect them, to ease all the hurts—past and present. The payoff came if they cared enough about you in return to want to do the same for you, too. A giving relationship. For the first time a clear picture of that kind of relationship for himself came to his mind—and the other person in the picture was Allyn.

But that didn't seem so strange when he hadn't been able to get the image of her out of his mind since he'd first laid eyes on her. And it was more than that. There was the lightness in his chest every time he saw her and the excitement whenever he thought of maneuvering some time with her. She was the first woman he had ever wanted in more than a surface way. The first woman he had ever met that had inspired thoughts that he could have what his father had had with his mother, what Mike had had with Emma.

Take care of Allyn? Yes, he wanted to take care of her, to soothe whatever old demons haunted her, to make her feel secure. But not because he believed she needed it. Because he cared for her. Strongly.

Thursday nights were Allyn's busiest. Several of her restaurant accounts only ordered desserts for their Friday, Saturday and Sunday business. Not baking for the office rounds on the weekend gave her the time for the extra Saturday and Sunday work, but there was no slack at all for Friday. In fact, Friday's office sales were always higher as dieters indulged in end-of-the-week rewards.

And this Thursday night Allyn was dragging. The usual week-ending fatigue wasn't the only cause. Her spirits were low, too. How could she actually miss Ian

Reed's company? One day together after a couple of impromptu dinners, and here she was feeling empty and alone.

"Lonesome," she mused to herself as she spread mousse into molds. "I haven't been lonesome the whole time I've been here. Until you came, Ian Reed. Now look at me. Even being busy and dead tired doesn't help."

There had to be a flaw in the man. There was always a flaw. She just had to look closer, and then she could put him out of her mind, reassured that she really didn't want anything to do with him.

Flaws. Flaws.

It wasn't in his easy nature. That humor of his was deadly to her controls. Obviously it wasn't in his appearance. If a more appealing man existed, Allyn had never met him. It wasn't in the way he treated her—who wouldn't like to be pursued to the extent that he even neglected his business to spend time with her?

His business. There was a flaw.

Allyn knew too well of one particular class distinction. A successful, educated man could not be satisfied for a prolonged amount of time with a less successful, uneducated woman. When the blush of attraction wore off, the woman became someone who didn't fit in, who just didn't know what was ultimately interesting and important.

And Ian Reed, a step above any successful, educated man she had ever encountered, was just one more step above Allyn. Ian's world might as well be English royalty for all she knew about what went on within its ranks. A major flaw indeed.

So why didn't it make her stop wishing he was here, dipping his finger in this brownie batter?

But wasn't the class difference only a problem in a long-term relationship? And she had no intention of ever being involved in one of those again. So didn't that make Ian Reed, with his globe-hopping occupation and his history as a bachelor, absolutely nonthreatening?

What was there to be afraid of? Why not enjoy it for what it's worth?

Good questions.

Just because everybody else—everybody else being Sylvia and Chris and the rest of the family—only thought in terms of finding a man and getting married again didn't mean Allyn had to think that way. In fact, she realized suddenly, her own thinking had always been at the two extremes—being totally alone or hunting for a second husband.

So what about something in between?

Seeing Ian Reed didn't interfere with her work. He was interesting, attractive, entertaining. She thoroughly liked his company. Why did being with him, liking to be with him for now, have to be anything more than that? She didn't have to let involvement, longevity, the threat of coming to need him, loom over her. Why couldn't she just have a fling? Date, let go a little, have a good time and still keep herself, her heart separate?

Of course she could.

Couldn't she?

Why did common sense always intrude in the form of a little voice raising ugly questions about just how vulnerable she might be?

Maybe because she had been so vulnerable before.

Maybe because she had not put that vulnerability to the test in two years.

But then, lessons were learned from harsh experiences. Of course she couldn't be certain she was strong enough to be immune to anything as debilitating as love. There were no guarantees. But she believed in herself, in her own strength, now. Ian Reed was a risk. Dangerous in his attraction and appeal. But less dangerous in the plain fact that his availability was limited to how long he could linger in Denver. That made him a calculated risk. So why not take it and enjoy the time, knowing it had an end?

One risk in two years. That wasn't such a gamble. There wasn't really anything to be afraid of.

Forewarned is forearmed.

Allyn didn't finish up until well after ten, but in spite of the time she felt the urge to indulge herself in a seldom-done pampering that paid attention to the usually neglected sensual pleasures.

First she took out a perfumed candle and set it on the coffee table, leaving its single flame the only light, its fresh smell of grasses and wildflowers to chase away the lingering scents of baking. A slight breeze blew through the high branches of two large maple trees outside her apartment, and the sound of their dry, crackling leaves softly rustling drew her to open one of the windows. No mere five-minute shower would do tonight. Instead she poured a liberal amount of bubble bath into the tub, filled it nearly to the rim and settled into a warm, wet nirvana.

With slow, lazy strokes she lathered her skin with the expensive, perfumed soap Chris had given her and sank down to rest her head and close her eyes. Luxury.

For twenty minutes she rested somewhere between fantasy and actual sleep.

Then a knock at the apartment door took her out of her reverie.

"Just a minute," she called as she hastily dried off and pulled on a thick, wraparound terry-cloth robe.

Ian was waiting patiently on the landing when she opened the door. He was dressed in a gray silk suit with a pale pink shirt and a rose-colored, Windsor-knotted tie. For a split second, Allyn appreciated the sight of him in that impeccably tailored suit as he devoured her bathrobed form with his eyes. Then he smiled, and the chill of being damp in the night air went away.

"You will never know how glad I was to see your lights still on."

She knew. If he was half as glad as she was to find him standing there, it was enough. When he reached a hand to the back of her neck, pulling her to him, pressing his mouth to hers in a light, greeting kiss, it seemed as natural as rain. Allyn didn't question it. She just enjoyed it.

"Can I come in for a few minutes?" he asked in an intimately husky voice that strummed a chord in the pit of her stomach.

"Sure," she answered, as if there were no reason to doubt it, stepping with him back into the warmth of the candlelit apartment.

"Were you expecting someone?" Ian asked with a note of possessiveness as his eyes scoured the place, the first time he had ever seen it in any but a serviceable mode.

Allyn laughed lightly but offered nothing more than a simple "No" that managed to sound honest and mysterious at the same time.

Ian hadn't a clue as to what was going on, but he didn't much care. This was a different side to Allyn—receptive, soft, lazy—and he liked it. A lot.

His arm stayed around her shoulders as they crossed to the daybed and sat down, so close their thighs formed a seam. With his free hand, Ian loosened his tie and tugged it off, tossing it to the coffee table.

"This is probably going to sound crazy, but I missed you today." He fingered the damp curls above her ear.

"Some say chocolate is addictive, but not in just one day's indulgence," she joked, feeling relaxed and as if every nerve were exposed in the nicest way.

"It's not the chocolate I'm addicted to." He leaned nearer. "You smell so good you're making my head light."

"Shall I move?" she flirted.

He pulled her in tight. "Not a chance. How was your day?" The words were commonplace but, affected by the environment she had created, his tone was deep, rich, intimate.

"Long. How was yours?" Allyn's voice, too, was soft in answer.

"Endless," he said against the side of her neck. "But I have Jon completely introduced and indoctrinated, so it was worth it." He straightened, intending to search her expression for signs of assurance that what was actually happening here was what he *thought* was happening, but her robe gaped slightly at the top, allowing him a shadowy view that just hinted at what was beneath. His gaze got stuck there until he forced it back up to her face.

Allyn saw where his attention was and the difficulty he had in altering it. A muscle tightened in his jaw, and she realized with a small amount of shock at herself, that her own mind was on the same track. Only for once rather than pushing down on these feelings she did nothing more than revel in them.

"I have a pretty fair collection of cognacs for the tortes. Would you like a glass?"

"Will you have one with me?"

"Maybe a little Grand Marnier." She padded barefoot to pour the liqueur while Ian took off his coat, removed his cufflinks and rolled the sleeves back just once.

"I wasn't sure you would let me in," he said, testing the change in her.

"I figured if I didn't you would just climb in a window."

"That wouldn't have mattered to you before, my reticent Ms. Danner."

Allyn only smiled a small, secretive smile. "Maybe I've cried uncle. You're nothing if not persistent."

When she came back he didn't hesitate to reach for her arm, pulling her close beside him again. Accepting the expensive liqueur in the Styrofoam cup, he peered comically into it. "Laced with arsenic to get rid of me for good?"

"A chance you'll have to take."

He took a sip, his eyes staying on her over the cup rim. "I think it's worth it." For a moment Ian only watched her. The golden glow of candlelight gilded her hair to glimmering bronze and left her face a play of soft, alluring shadows and glistening cream. The natural simplicity of her beauty took his breath away. "I like this," he ventured carefully, his deep voice lapping out at her like the lure of a warm ocean wave. "But then, I like everything about you."

Allyn just smiled, as contented as a Cheshire cat. She was warm and so relaxed. And nothing had ever seemed more right than being here like this with him. "I thought you were just masochistic," she teased in a way that made it sound seductive.

"Sometimes in this past week I've wondered that, myself. But everything was worth it to come in here tonight and find you...soft and welcoming...." Still fearing he was misreading the signs, Ian said, "About last night..."

But Allyn's memory of the past night was not in the parting. It was in the feel of his mouth on hers, of his body against hers, of her own needs, aroused and left unsatisfied. "I guess the intensity of my own feelings made me panic," she confessed.

"You don't seem panicked now."

"I'm not," she answered easily, realizing only as she said the words that they were true. Instinct told her the time was right. She wanted him. There was no reason to question it.

Silence fell, but the air between them was charged. He caressed the side of her face with the back of his hand, looking intently into her eyes. The surface of her skin tingled with life.

"Strange lady that you are—" his voice was a husky whisper "—I have the sense that if I even mention what I'm feeling about you I'm going to scare you away. But know this, you are...special...to me."

He was so close that Allyn could see the light stubble of a day's growth of beard on his angular face. The smell of the perfumed candle wafted around them. Her body was alive with desire. "Make love to me...." It was part request, part statement.

Ian drew a deep breath, as if he had been granted something he desperately wanted and hadn't expected to get. He was suddenly very, very serious. "Be sure, love."

She only breathed a little laugh at that and answered with her eyes delving deeply into his, devouring his extraordinarily handsome face. "I am," she said without a pause.

Ian stood then and took her with him. He pulled the thick quilt from the daybed and, after stepping over the coffee table, spread it in the open center of the floor, making the candlelight flicker wildly before it settled again to throw long shadows across the downy nest.

He kicked off his shoes and socks, tugged his shirt from his pants and unbuttoned it, leaving it hanging like curtains on either side of his exquisite male chest and hard belly.

Allyn wanted him. Her whole body wanted him. Nothing else mattered at that moment.

She took a long, deep, strengthening breath and went to him as he tossed his shirt away and unfastened his slacks. Without thinking about it, Allyn reached for him, laying her palms against the honed mounds of his pectorals, reveling in the feel of his skin and chest hair over hardened muscles. And when she looked up he smiled down at her with only one side of his mouth, a welcoming, pleased expression softening his face.

He leaned to kiss the side of her neck, nipping lightly with his teeth as he kicked away the last of his clothes. His deft hands pulled the sash of her robe free and then slid inside and over her shoulders so the terry-cloth garment fell behind her, the last barrier separating them. His big hands against her small, taut back, he pressed her into him, and that first meeting of bare skin electrified Allyn's nerve endings. Every inch of her screamed out for him—for his touch, for the feel of his desire, hard and powerful against her.

From outside, autumn leaves played an ethereal symphony in the wind. The dim glow of yellow light gilded their naked bodies as he pulled her with him to lie on the quilt. "You are too beautiful to believe," he whispered into the still-damp curls atop her head, and his words fed a starving place deep inside her.

Their lips met, mingling breath of orange liqueur, teasing and exploring and testing the tips of teeth and the contours of velvety caverns with tongues emboldened by passion. And then Ian pulled back to find her nipple with his mouth and hand at once, and Allyn's back arched in pure, pleasured response. The feeling was as new as if it were the first time, sending hot sparks through her veins. She clasped his head, combing through the thick softness of his sable hair. Bliss and desperate hunger at once coursed through her.

Her hands eagerly sought the feel of him, of bulging biceps and hair-roughened forearms, of the mounds and recesses of the straining muscles that rippled across his back, of pectorals that shifted with the movement of his own hands on her and male nipples that hardened to tiny kernels beneath her fingers. Her mouth explored the tense cords of his neck and the deep hollow of his throat, teasing the sharp ridge of his collarbone with the flick of her tongue as her hands became less timid and skipped to the bolelike thickness of his thighs. He was magnificent. Incredible. Wonderful. And she wanted him, all of him, with a desire that left her weak.

The tiny, gentle nips of his teeth and pinches of large, tender fingers at her nipples tightened a cord that stretched to the center of her. And just when she thought she could bear no more, his mouth teased a path down her flat stomach and then lower still. Warm and wet and more wonderful than all that had come before, Allyn writhed and thought she might burst with pleasure. "Now." The word barely escaped her throat.

He came into her so slowly, so carefully, ignoring the striving arch of her spine and the demand of her hands. To Allyn it seemed like an eternity before he had filled her completely, in the way her body craved. Still cautious, still considerate, he only pulsed within her at first, finding her mouth with his tongue to trace her lips and torment her with kisses, reaching her breast with his hand to roll her nipple between his fingers until her need was so great her hips matched the pulsing of him inside of her beat by beat. And then he began, thrusting with a steady rhythm, building stronger, deeper, faster, until white-hot lights exploded in Allyn as if he had opened floodgates too long closed and locked. Her fingers dug into his back, holding him as he found the peak with her, and their bodies melded together.

And then every nerve, every muscle, wound down. Where there had been so many sounds of passion, now there was silence, broken only by softly labored breathing and the beat of Ian's heart beneath Allyn's ear as she lay beside him. Where there had been tendons and sinews taut with need there were arms and legs too heavy to move. Where there had been frantic need there was now satiety. First alive and alert and energized as if they had both been electrically charged, Ian and Allyn now were spent, leaden with fatigue.

With one arm holding Allyn at his side, her head on his chest, Ian reached for the quilt, pulled it around them, and they both slept.

Chapter Seven

When Allyn's alarm went off at three Friday morning, she burst up as if she'd been shot from a cannon. Her bearings were off, and it took a minute to locate the loudly buzzing clock. Once it had been silenced, she collapsed on the floor beside the coffee table to actually wake up.

From the quilt out of which she had just bounded, Ian groaned and rolled over. That was when Allyn remembered he was there. She was naked. Three hours before they had made love and fallen asleep.

A surge of adrenaline woke her all the way up in a hurry. Her eyes came open like window shades on overwound springs as she looked around for her bathrobe. Finding it, she flipped it over her shoulders and hotfooted it to the bathroom, where she closed the door, careful not to make a sound, then fell back against it.

So much for two years of caution.

Post-passion panic. That's what you get when you don't have a date or even talk to a man who isn't your father, brother, boss or landlord for two years, and then hormones lead you into bed with one.

It had been nice, though....

Allyn snapped her wandering thoughts to attention. The only thing to do was to go on as if nothing had happened. A biological need had been satisfied. No big deal. No big deal at all. Just get dressed—thank goodness she always left clean clothes for the next day in the bathroom so she could dress quickly in the warmth of that small space—and forget it.

Taking her own advice, she hung her bathrobe on the hook behind the door, took a quick shower and slipped into blue jeans and a fluorescent orange sweatshirt. Then she turned to the mirror above the sink. Did her lips still look a little puffy from lovemaking? Maybe it was just her imagination. But they were redder. She applied extraheavy gloss, hoping it would hide the color, but all it did was enhance it. And her cheeks. This must be what was meant by the blush of love. She grimaced and tried a little face powder, but the roses in her cheeks shone through. *I look like an advertisement for the benefits of a healthy romp. I'm a walking neon sign.*

But there was no help for it, so she fluffed the tight curls of her hair, took a deep breath and forged back into the apartment.

Ian was still asleep.

Allyn tiptoed to the other side of the island kitchen counter and turned on only the light above the stove, watching him from a distance as if he were an extraterrestrial.

Up and at 'em. Rise and shine. Get out of here so I can forget what happened and how much I'd like it to

happen again, she thought. But she didn't say anything.

What did people do in these situations? She supposed it would be too tacky to shuffle him out onto the
landing and then throw his clothes after him. Breakfast in bed was probably the classiest way to wake up a
lover. But he wasn't in bed; he was in the middle of the
floor. And she didn't have anything to serve him for
breakfast. She didn't own any coffee at all, let alone the
specially blended brand he liked.

She cleared her throat as loudly as she could manage, hoping that that would do it. It didn't. He just
raised his arm in an arch over his head, exposing his
bare chest above the quilt. Allyn looked away, her fin-
gertips tapping a rapid dance on the countertop.

Ignore him, she advised herself. Go about your business. Act as if nothing had happened. Isn't that what
modern morality dictates? Bounce into bed, bounce out
again and go back to work?

Allyn turned on the ovens and began taking her pre-
mixed doughs from the refrigerators. It wasn't easy
keeping her eyes off Ian, but she managed.

Without any attempt to keep the clatter of spoons
against bowls and pans against racks quiet, Ian only
slept about another fifteen minutes. Then he appeared
on the other side of the counter, the quilt wrapped
around his waist.

When Allyn didn't acknowledge him in any way, Ian
said, "I may be wrong, but I think the most common
course here is to say good-morning. At least techni-
cally, it's morning. From the way you're banging those
pans around I'm not too sure about the good part. But
I'll start the ball rolling anyway. Good morning, Allyn."

"Morning," she answered curtly.

"Uh-huh. Like that, is it? I was afraid this would happen: regrets."

"I don't have any regrets," she said as she worked, sparing him not so much as a glance.

"Great. Then how about an encore?" he challenged.

It was a good thing he didn't realize how tempting that sounded. "Sorry, I'm running late as it is."

"Why is it that the words sound smooth but the actions look agitated?"

"Maybe because I mean what I say. But I'm in a hurry."

He came around the counter and stopped her in midstride on her way to put cake pans in the oven. "Hey, I need a little reassurance here."

Allyn had no choice but to look up at him. His hair was sleep-tousled, his square jaw shadowed with beard stubble. Lord, even unkempt, he was gorgeous! And how come the feel of his hand on her arm still shot electric shocks through her? Shouldn't familiarity and satiety have neutralized those effects? But then who was satiated? Not her. She wanted him as much at that moment as she had several hours before. Practicality kept it contained, but the desire softened her. "I didn't think men needed reassurance."

"I'd cut off my right arm rather than blow things with you. Did making love to you do that?"

"It's not that," she said quietly. "I...didn't know what morning-after protocol was. And I really do have to get to work. Friday is my worst day."

"'Morning-after protocol'? Do you think there's a handbook?"

"For all I know..."

Ian chuckled, shook his head and pressed a light kiss to her lips, deciding to let the subject drop. "I didn't come over here last night with the express purpose of getting you into bed. I had something to tell you."

"Can I put these pans in the oven first?" *And get farther away from you before I forget I can't possibly crawl back under that quilt with you?*

He released her arm and disappeared into the bathroom. When he came out he had pulled on his pants, but the sight of his still-bare torso kept Allyn's nerve endings alive. She busied herself pouring a cupful of tea and offering it to him when he came over to lean against the counter. He crossed his arms on his chest and turned up his nose. "That stuff smells like chewing gum."

She shrugged and took back her offering, taking a sip of it herself. "It's mint tea."

"I'll pass."

"You had something to say," she reminded, hoping he would get it out and leave her poor raging senses in peace.

"Right. And it's going to sound heavy-handed— mostly because it is. I've arranged to spend this weekend showing you that there's more in life than chocolate that can be divinely decadent."

"*You*'ve arranged to spend the weekend? I spend my weekends working."

"Outraged in an instant. Do you have quick-tempered Irish blood running in your veins, Ms. Danner? Never mind. That was a rhetorical question. I never had a doubt that you spend your weekends working. I did a little checking and this is what I've done—get ready to explode. I called all of your accounts—so handy of you to keep a full list there on the inside of that cupboard—and told them you had a family emergency that had taken you away."

For a moment Allyn was dumbstruck. Then she said very quietly, full of disbelief, "You did what?"

"You heard me." There was a firmness to his voice, a take-charge tone that she had never heard before... and didn't particularly like. She tried to hold onto her temper as he went on. "Most of your clients were very understanding, especially when I assured them you had not left them in the lurch. They were more than happy to compromise a little freshness to still have Danner's Decadent Desserts to serve this weekend. So this is what I've arranged. Jon will be here later and the three of us are going to work straight through the day making goodies. I hired a professional service—complete with girls who will make your office rounds—to deliver all three days' worth of orders today, and then you and I will be off."

"I can't afford a delivery service," she shouted. So much for holding her temper.

"I didn't say *you* had hired them, I said *I* had. The entire weekend is on me."

"No, thanks." Allyn put her cup down on the counter so hard that tea splashed over the sides. Her blue eyes shot sparks at Ian. "You have a lot of nerve, Reed."

"And you need a rest, Danner." He was undaunted.

"No way. I can't believe you. Who do you think you are, to just take over like this?"

Ian sighed, patiently, but as if there were no question that the situation was in his control. "If I had asked you first, even under the same terms, would you have accepted?"

"Of course not."

"And when is the last time you had a break?" he asked reasonably.

"That doesn't matter. I'm not a child who needs to be forced to rest. And you're not my father—or anyone else, for that matter whose job it is to take care of me." Allyn paced to vent her anger while Ian calmly watched her.

"Good grief!" she spewed. "Are you this determined to get your own way in everything? You bulldoze your way into my life, my business—and now this!"

"Tell me you can't use a rest."

"Not at the expense of my business, I can't," she shouted.

"It isn't at the expense of your business," he answered reasonably. "Look, I apologize for the tactics—I told you it was heavy-handed. But I've seen how hard you work. I'll bet there isn't another soul who can say that. And you've been at this pace for what—a year, two? You drive yourself harder than anyone I have ever known, and it's potentially hazardous to your health, your well-being, your sanity and even your business. I want to give you a couple of days relief. That's all."

His genuine concern took some of the wind out of her sails. Allyn stopped pacing and stood with her forehead pressed against an upper cupboard, staring down at the counter as she thought about it.

Ian came to her, leaning his hips against the same counter, very near to her but not touching her. His voice was gentle, quiet, soothing. "I already have everything arranged so that absolutely no detriment will come out of this. We can drive to Colorado Springs when we finish up here. I have a suite—a two-bedroom suite—reserved at the Clarion Hotel there. Saturday and Sunday we can swim, golf, hike, take in the zoo—you name it. Elegant dinners, dancing in the evenings—whatever we can find to do, eat or buy that is as outrageously extravagant as that little city has to offer.''

All right, so it was tempting. But Allyn was still feeling contrary. ''No. Fancy-dress clothes are part of what I sold to raise the money I needed for my equipment. I don't own anything to wear to an elegant dinner. Taco Bell is as classy as I get.''

''Then we'll do it casually. The most important thing is that we get away from this ridiculous schedule you keep, relax and spend time together.''

Her defenses weakened, but she didn't let it show. ''I can't. I have to attend the baptism of my new niece on Sunday.''

''Not until three. We'll be back in time for that.''

With her head still against the cupboard she swiveled it to face him. ''How did you know that?'' Then it occurred to her, and she went back to staring at the counter. ''Don't tell me. My sister Chris called you.''

''I thought it was very nice of her to include me.''

''You think you're really smart, don't you, Reed? You know, must bullies don't wear silk suits.''

''All the bases are covered, love. In fact, both your sister and your friend Sylvia were so glad to hear you'd have a little R and R that if you refuse and I just forcibly abduct you and keep you prisoner—something I'm not at all adverse to—there isn't a soul who would alert the authorities to rescue you. You're stuck.''

The timer went off. Allyn grabbed up hot pads and flung the oven doors open. Ian's silence left her to think about the weekend he proposed. She wouldn't lose any business. She could definitely use a break—she had worked seven days a week since she began Danner's

Decadent Desserts. His intentions had been good; only his methods were rotten. It was a nice idea....

And she would be with Ian.

If she was going to have a fling, why not do it completely? said a little voice in the back of her mind.

With a flourishy flick of the wrist, and a still-peeved sigh of resignation, she slid a cookie sheet onto a cooling rack. "Okay, hotshot. You're on." She picked up the spatula, but before she used it to remove the fat brown delights from the pan she poked the air just in front of Ian with it to accentuate her point. "But know this, Reed. I don't appreciate being manipulated. My life, my business, are just that—mine—my domain. And no one rules that domain but me. Stick your meddling mitts into it again and you'll pull back stubs—no matter how good your intentions. Got that?"

Ian tried not to smile at her ferocity even though it struck him as comical. "Understood."

She nodded toward the trousers he wore. "All right then. You can't bake in a silk suit. Go dig out your real work clothes."

He reached one hand to the back of her neck to pull her into a second kiss. "You've made me a happy man."

She smiled slyly. "Not until three days' worth of desserts are baked and on their way out of here."

"And we're holed up in a champagne-filled hotel room. I'll be back in twenty minutes."

Allyn watched him remake the daybed and gather his clothes before he left. When he had gone, she wilted a little, wondering if it was wise to have let him get away with this. If it was wise to go at all, when her feelings for him were so strong.

But then that little voice asked what harm one weekend of relaxation could do.

Famous last words.

At seven-fifteen that morning Allyn and Ian watched the first delivery van drive away. Allyn's gaze followed like a worried mother's after the school bus on the first day. As the delivery truck pulled out a silver limousine appeared around the house and stopped in front of them.

Without aid of the chauffeur the rear door opened, and out stepped Jon Wyatt. Allyn stifled a laugh. He reminded her of a short, round teddy bear dressed in a V-necked white undershirt and sweatpants—not exactly what you'd expect to emerge from a limousine.

"Allyn Danner, meet my partner, Jon Wyatt."

"I'm all yours," Jon announced grandly, his arms outstretched in surrender.

Ian bent to whisper an aside in Allyn's ear. "He's also a gourmet cook. Taught me all I know."

"I hope it wasn't all he knew. Another one like you in my kitchen would be more of a liability than an asset," she teased, referring to the pan of brownies he had dropped on the floor in response to burning himself again.

Jon sniffed the air. "I think I can find my own way, if you two want to stand out here and waste time." His nose stayed in use all the way into the apartment. "If there is a heaven, I know it smells like this."

"Wait until you taste this stuff," Ian said proudly, causing a warm rush to go through Allyn.

She hid it by playing taskmaster. "Hey, I don't pay you two to stand around and chatter."

"She's paying us?" Jon raised eyebrows that spiked up his forehead, looked askance at the apartment and teased, "I would have never guessed she could afford our two-fifty-an-hour rate."

"Two dollars and fifty cents? A pittance," she said, playing along. "You guys must be some kind of investors to split two-fifty an hour and ride around in limousines."

Ian laughed. "*Two hundred and fifty dollars*, love. And if we work together that's each, not split."

Allyn cocked her head back in shock. "Is that the truth? Do you actually charge two hundred and fifty dollars an hour?"

"Sometimes we work on a percentage basis and it works out to be more." This from Jon, amused by her surprise.

Allyn blew out a breath as if she had been hit in the stomach. "I'm definitely in the wrong business."

"Not from the way this place smells, you aren't." Jon began to prowl the kitchen. "And if I don't get a taste of something soon I *am* going to send you a bill."

Ian made coffee and they took a few minutes' break before getting back to work. Jon ate one of every kind of cookie and each variation of the chocolate muffins—enough to weigh King Kong down for hours. But when his splurge was over and everything had been judged the most delicious he had ever eaten, he went to work with energy to equal Allyn's, never taking another taste of dough or dipping a finger in the batter the way Ian was wont to do.

As the day progressed they made an efficient team. Allyn did all the measuring and mixing, leaving unspoken the fact that she was protecting her recipes. Ian was left the easiest tasks of simply greasing pans, stirring ingredients and wrapping the finished products, while Jon was adept at forming the cookies, knowing just the right amount of batter to be spread into pans, and removing delicate cakes and cookies to cool. Jon was also proficient with frosting the tortes, leaving Allyn only the need to decorate them when they were completely assembled.

Pleased and amazed at how much help the shorter man was, Allyn paused behind Ian as he fumbled with plastic wrap to whisper, "Roping Jon into this was a smart move, Reed."

Ian smiled back over his shoulder at her. "I'm nobody's fool, *Danner*. What is it going to take to get you to call me by my first name, for crying out loud?"

"I don't know. For a man who makes upward of two hundred and fifty dollars an hour it seems to me it should be *Mr.* Reed. Would you like that better?"

"No, I would not like that better," he parroted through a playfully menacing snarl.

Just then Jon called for her help. As she moved away, Allyn taunted, "Back to work, Reed."

"I'm going to make it my goal for this weekend to get you to say it at least once," he said to her departing back.

Throughout the day, the mood was light and jovial. Jon shared the same sense of humor that united Allyn and Ian, and time went fast. But more than the simple pleasure she found in the company and the banter, the day was an even better demonstration than having only Ian's help, as well as giving her an indication of the difference between having assistance from someone who knew his way around a kitchen.

Productivity was high, and Allyn decided that she could triple her business even in her small kitchen with a little help and someone else to deliver. With a larger kitchen, more ovens, even a small staff and a few delivery people, she would be well on her way to owning a successful business, to reaching her goals.

The last delivery van was loaded and ready by four that afternoon. Jon put in a call for the return of the limousine to pick him up, and when it arrived he pecked a friendly kiss on Allyn's cheek, slapped Ian on the back and said as he departed, "I leave you to your weekend, kids."

"Who was that masked man?" Allyn deadpanned as they watched him get back into the long silver car.

Ian snaked an arm around her shoulders and squeezed. "The answer to my prayers, because this means I can have you all to myself. How long before you're ready to leave?"

Butterflies took flight in Allyn's stomach. Tension or anticipation? A little of both, she decided. But there wasn't even a thought of refusing. "An hour?"

"Perfect." Just before he let go of her, Ian licked a drop of brownie batter from the side of her nose in a way that was terribly sensual.

And the butterflies fluttered a little lower than her stomach.

The car Ian rented for the drive to Colorado Springs was a wine-colored Mercedes. The tan interior still smelled new, and the leather seats were so soft and comfortable that Allyn sank down in the passenger side and promptly fell asleep.

Periodically as he drove, Ian glanced over at her peaceful profile, her high cheekbones dusted with rose, her lips slightly, provocatively, parted. But his thoughts were on her more than periodically. She seemed to have taken up permanent residence there.

Interstate 25 stretched out before him, and Ian's inclination was to keep going, to take Allyn completely away from her work, her past, to free her from everything, to take care of her, pamper her, love her. . . .

Softly, almost silently, he laughed at himself. It was love all right. And that explained his need to protect her, to take care of her. He loved Allyn Danner.

Marriage was his next thought, which surprised even himself. But once the surprise faded, he let the idea grow. He wouldn't want a "designer" marriage—those where the husband and wife led separate lives, coming together at Christmas and tax time. An old-fashioned marriage was the only kind he could see for himself. And suddenly he saw it quite clearly—with Allyn.

The self-absorption of being a goal-oriented professional person was a necessary component in accomplishing those goals. But it could easily become a whole way of life. He had been alone—rootless, disconnected—long enough to realize that the same self-absorption didn't make for eternal happiness; that ultimately it was a lonely, shallow, empty existence. Okay, so it was a cliché, but success, money, everything money could buy, really were only wonderful if they were shared with someone you cared about, someone you were bonded with. Life was easier, more comfortable, with money and success, but it was only enriched with love, with the shared enjoyment of a full partner. What he wanted, he knew now, was Allyn as that partner— the kind of partner Emma had been for Mike, the kind Ian's mother had been for his father.

Suddenly it seemed like a foregone conclusion that he and Allyn would marry.

And in his mind the only thing left was to open Allyn's eyes to that foregone conclusion.

While Ian registered at the front desk of the Clarion Hotel, Allyn tried to look nonchalant. Curbing the urge to whistle softly to prove she was taking her first coming-to-a-hotel-to-have-an-affair in her stride, she paced the lobby.

Looking at the Indian motif of the hotel's decorations, she pretended a deep interest in macramé wall hangings and clay pots holding pussy willows. She dodged the potted plants that stood along the decorative adobe wall surrounding the fireplace and sitting area, lest she dive behind one and give herself away. *Two rooms,* she wanted to say to everyone who even glanced her way. *We're taking a suite with two bedrooms.* Sure you are: she imagined the sarcastic answer she was certain would come, *and the moon is made of green cheese, there really is a Santa Claus and if you blow your nose in public, nobody notices.*

Allyn plunged her left hand into the pocket of her khaki slacks so her ringless finger wouldn't show. *You're hopeless, Danner. Hopeless.*

She tried not to slouch on the way to the room.

The suite's foyer opened into a living area done in stately hunter-green and ivory, a velvet sofa and two wing chairs. A carved pedestal table stood before a large picture window that framed a picturesque view of the Rocky Mountains. From opposite sides of the room opened the doors to the two bedrooms, each with separate baths. Allyn said a silent thanks for the privacy that was available if she so chose. At that moment it seemed likely that she would.

Ian tipped the bellboy and closed the door after him, and Allyn felt as awkward as if she were a mail-order bride on her wedding night. Discovering a silver tray on the low coffee table, she bent to investigate. Waiting were caviar, shrimp, oysters, three cheeses, strawberries, olives in the center of carrot tulips, an apple sliced into a swan and decorated with slivered almonds, melon slices, cauliflower and broccoli, a bottle of champagne and two fluted glasses.

She took an olive and popped it into her mouth. "There's enough food here for the whole weekend. Did you plan to keep me prisoner?"

He grinned. "Could I get away with it?"

"And miss the zoo? Not on a bet. I'm a sucker for the cat house." She grimaced at her own words, but Ian only laughed.

"My father warned me to stay away from cathouses," he teased as he poured the champagne and handed her a glass. Moving the tray to the very end of the oblong coffee table, he sat directly in front of her. "We came here to relax, remember? You don't seem to be doing much of that. Second thoughts?"

"Who, me?"

He cast her a sly, knowing glance as he stood and crossed to the door of the bedroom that was to be hers. With the door open, he made an elaborate show of locking and unlocking the inch-thick deadbolt. "One firm *no* will get you an undisturbed eight hours' sleep all by yourself. But just in case you have doubts, this lock guarantees it. You won't hear a complaint or a recrimination out of me. Okay? Now, have some caviar." He came back to sit on the coffee table.

Allyn felt only marginally better. She decided there was nothing to do but take this weekend as it came. Too late to back out now. She wrinkled her nose at his suggestion. "I make it a policy never to eat fish ova, thank you very much."

"Try this, then. Our dinner reservations aren't for another two hours." He dipped a strawberry in his champagne and reached to feed it to her. Allyn felt hot again. The man was better than an electric blanket. Then all at once she just resolved to let go. She was here, she enjoyed him. It was the first fun she'd had in far too long. Why not?

She smiled, slowly, seductively, and ate the strawberry from his fingers. "You know, Reed," she teased, "I don't think you're good for me."

When it came to dress clothes, Allyn had not been understating when she said she didn't have a thing to wear. She literally didn't. An antique lace blouse was the single fancy article she had retained from the sale of all but the most essential of her belongings. Coupled with plain, although crisply pressed, brown slacks, it was the best she could do.

Knowing the outfit was going to need some sort of accessory, she had purloined several small rose-colored straw flowers from a basket in Emma's kitchen and picked some baby's breath from Emma's garden just before leaving home. Using a thread from the handy little sewing kit provided by the hotel, she fashioned the flowers into a small cluster. Buttoning the high collar of the blouse all the way to her chin, she pinned the tiny makeshift corsage at her throat and stood back from the mirror to see if it had worked.

Not bad, she judged. Heads would not turn in awe, but it would do.

If the dress code of Bolero's—the most elegant of the Clarion's restaurants—was coats and ties, nothing was said. And if Ian noticed that he and Allyn were the only people in the place dressed so casually, he didn't show it. But as they dined on vichyssoise, fresh spinach salad, mesquite-broiled red snapper and wild rice, Allyn's self-conscious glance strayed to the more formally garbed patrons.

"Why are you so on edge tonight? You look as if we're clandestine lovers and you're watching for your husband to come in at any moment and catch us."

Allyn yanked her gaze from a haughty old woman in chiffon. "It's just that I think we're slightly under-dressed," she whispered.

He poured her more wine and spoke in a normal voice. "How can a woman who lives in jeans and sweatshirts worry so much about wearing the right clothes? You are a constant source of paradoxes, Ms. Danner."

"Just because I don't own them, doesn't mean I don't know which clothes are right and wrong in any given situation."

He studied her for a moment. It wasn't vanity, he was sure of that. "Do you know what I think?"

"Is it something I want to know?"

He ignored her question. "I think that somewhere, someone has left you with a whole bundle of high-octane doubts about yourself—beauty, brains, appeal, worth—everything. I have the feeling that you see yourself through the eyes of some person who was ig-norant enough to have rejected you." Ian reached to tilt her chin from staring at the lady in chiffon again, forc-ing her gaze to meet his. Very softly he said, "If you can't see yourself through your own eyes, then try looking through mine instead. Because they appreciate what they see. All of what they see. Inside and out. With clothes—any clothes—or without.''

Allyn felt the heat of color rise up her neck and suffuse her face. She carefully removed his hand from her chin. "Thanks, but compliments make me blush, and there are few more unsightly things than a red-faced redhead," she joked. Then, to change the subject, she blurted, "So tell me, Reed. Why haven't you ever been married?"

He shook his head and laughed a little at her obvious discomfort, before conceding the change. "I know, it raises eyebrows." He mimicked, "Thirty-five and never been married? Is he normal?"

Allyn toyed with her earlobe. "That thought never crossed my mind."

"Damn. I was hoping to have a good reason to prove my virility tonight."

"I'm taking note of the fact that you still haven't answered my question. Why haven't you ever married?"

"Career obsession. I was committed to mine, and I knew no marriage could survive the travel, the late hours, the intensity."

"I see," she said a bit tightly.

The edge of condemnation in her tone confused Ian. Without his understanding why he felt the need to defend himself. "It was a lot like what you're doing right now—putting the rest of your life on hold until you make a success of your job. Not expecting anyone else to sacrifice for your goals."

She thought about that perspective for a moment and then smiled. "You're right."

He frowned at her. "Why did I feel as if I'd said something wrong until I made that analogy?"

"I don't know. Why did you?"

He watched her carefully. "It came from you. But I can't put my finger on why."

"A shrink would say a guilty conscience is making you defensive and you're reading into it something perfectly innocent on my part."

Still he watched her. "You're very good at that, aren't you?"

"At being innocent?" she asked innocently.

"At being evasive. It strikes me that I know very little about your past, about the experiences that go into making Allyn Danner. And every time I get what might be a peek and probe a little, you avoid it."

"Don't be silly." She took her napkin from her lap, half hid a yawn behind it and then left it in a little rumple on the table. "I don't know about you, but I'm beat. Would you mind making this an early night? Then I'll be bright-eyed for tomorrow."

He saw through her. But the weekend was intended for pleasure and relaxation, so after a moment of studying her as if it might offer some clue, he let her have her evasion. "It's a deal," he conceded, pushing his chair out and rounding the table to help her up. There would be other times, he told himself as they left the restaurant. Sooner or later he was going to find out what made Ms. Danner tick.

The walk to their suite was quiet. Ian's hand rode her waist all the way, and Allyn debated with herself on how she was going to let this evening end. When he closed the door behind them and turned her in his arms she still hadn't decided.

His hands rubbed up and down her arms, slowly and with just enough pressure to ignite a tingling sensation along the surface of her skin. In the dim light of a single table lamp coming from the living room Allyn could see the seriousness in his black eyes as he captured her glance and held it.

"I . . . care for you, Allyn," he said softly, the depth of his tone saying more than the words.

Then his mouth lowered to hers, at first lightly, again and again, tenderly taking her lips between his, letting his tongue trace the silkiness just inside.

Allyn's eyes drifted closed, heavily, weighted with the sudden surge of desire. He smelled spicy and tasted of the fruit sorbet they'd had for dessert. A warm glow started deep inside her and swelled as his kiss deepened and his arms encircled her, pulling her in close against him, flattening her breasts against the hardness of his chest. Instantly awakened, her body craved him as intensely as it had the previous night—maybe more, now that the memory of lovemaking was fresh. The thought of being led off to the bedroom, of feeling his hands and mouth explore her body, of reveling in the exploration of his, erupted such a yearning need in her.

Ian felt her yield in the molding of her body to his. Taking his lips from hers he bent and swept her up into his arms.

Like a cold shower, that very action set off alarms in her mind. To be carried like a child, completely under his control, made her feel helpless, powerless. To Allyn no worse feeling existed. Suddenly she could think only that Ian had had control of this whole day, of this whole evening, of this whole situation, maybe of this whole relationship. It sent a wave of panic through her. And a surging need to regain some of that control.

"I can't!" she blurted before he had crossed the threshold to his room.

The urgency in her voice stopped him. Ian looked down at her, seeing the tension in her features and not knowing what had put it there. "Allyn?" was all he said.

"Put me down," she ordered.

He did. "What happened?"

How could she explain? She wanted him. Desperately. And yet the very scene other women would find so romantic threw her into a tailspin of emotions. Nervously she stepped away from him, going to fidget with a velvet pillow she took from the couch. "Just...not tonight."

Baffled and concerned, Ian moved to her, but when she nearly jumped away he stopped. "Did I misread the signs?"

"No. I guess I just changed my mind." As if she had successfully completed her mission to fluff the sofa pillows to perfection she faced him, not quite looking him in the eye. "Let's not talk about it. I'm really tired—and you should be, too. I know it's probably archaic and silly, but I feel the need for a solitary night's rest."

Ian watched her from beneath a deep frown, knowing full well she was hiding whatever it was that had cooled the passion he had felt in her. "What piece am I missing from the puzzle of Allyn Danner?"

The piece that says after being bulldozed she needs a little space, she thought but couldn't say. Instead she headed for her own bedroom. "There are no missing pieces because I'm not a puzzle. But I like the illusion of being a mystery woman, so I'll let you wonder," she said glibly.

"Allyn..." His deep, solemn voice stopped her at her door.

She turned, one hand holding onto the knob as if it were a lifeline while she forced an innocently questioning expression to her face.

Ian hesitated, thought twice about forcing the issue, and discarded his own need for persisting until he found out everything he wanted to know. "Tomorrow to the zoo? Or would you rather go home?"

Just giving her the choice made her feel better. "The zoo," she said and then relaxed enough to sound genuine for the first time since she had nearly leaped out of his arms. "It's only that I need some time alone tonight. No big deal. Really."

He was dubious, and it showed. But he nodded his acceptance of it and said, "Sleep well, love."

"You, too," she answered and escaped to her room.

Behind the closed door Allyn felt the rebellion of her body against the decision to refuse her own desire and knew a moment of doubt about it. But in the end she stayed alone because ultimately she preferred self-denial to losing her own sense of control. She could live with raging, unsatisfied emotions. But life without the power to control what happened to her was something else entirely.

Chapter Eight

Old habits die hard. Even without the herald of the alarm clock, Allyn woke up at three on Saturday morning. Berating herself, she lay in her king-size bed, her eyes stubbornly closed, and tried to go back to sleep. Her first chance in two years to sleep until dawn and her body wouldn't cooperate. Go figure.

When her thoughts wandered to estimates of how big a dessert account the Clarion Hotel could be, of how much the delivery service would charge for a daily run to Colorado Springs, and of actually hunting up the night manager and approaching him with the possibility of Danner's Decadent Desserts supplying them, she knew she was never going to go back to sleep.

"This is a vacation, remember, Danner?" she whispered to herself. So what would qualify as a divinely decadent vacation at three-thirty in the morning?

She decided on a cup of tea sipped while lazing in the center of this exquisitely comfortable, gigantic bed, propped among all six pillows watching television. Maybe not divine or decadent by anyone else's standards, but appealing to her all the same. There was something to be said for simple pleasures.

It didn't occur to her to call room service. Instead she pulled on the pants and sweater of the previous day, slipped on her shoes and snuck like a thief in the night out of the room.

The hall was so quiet that the ping of the arriving elevator seemed to echo. In the lobby the night manager was doing paperwork and a bellboy snored softly behind the desk. Just off the lobby The Deli was open round-the-clock. It was there she headed.

Hot coffee steamed from a full pot, but for tea Allyn had to wait while the water heated. As she did, she scanned the display counter to gauge how her own confections compared with those the Clarion had for sale. Hers would be an improvement, she decided. Crossing the lobby on her way back to the suite, Allyn smiled a good-morning at the manager, pretending not to notice his are-you-out-of-your-mind expression and resisting the urge to talk desserts—an account like the Clarion was out of her league at present. But she would keep it in mind when she expanded.

Back in her room she shed her clothes, fluffed the pillows and ensconced herself in the bed with her teacup in one hand and the TV's remote control in the other. Flipping through the cable fed channels she found the movie *The Rainmaker* just beginning. Burt Lancaster and Katharine Hepburn. Pure gold. Allyn settled in as contentedly as if she had the world at her feet.

Not only was Katharine Hepburn her all-time favorite actress, but Allyn admired her as a strong, independent woman—unlike the Lizzie character she portrayed in *The Rainmaker*. Lizzie was desperate to find a husband. In her little world, to be an old maid was the same as being a leper. Maybe worse.

Allyn would rather have seen herself relating to the strong, independent Katharine Hepburn than to the lonely, desperate Lizzie, but she realized that she had a certain amount of understanding of Lizzie's not wanting to spend her life alone—no matter what she told Sylvia to the contrary. Not that being alone was so bad, she reminded herself. She was too busy to be lonely and if she ever was, she could always call someone—her sister, Sylvia, friends. And as long as their husbands didn't mind or have anything else planned, they would provide company. Maybe not companionship. But company.

Anyway, there wasn't all that much loneliness. Better that than betrayal.

Chuck the husband hunting and just have a good time with old Starbuck, Lizzie. That's what I'm doing with Ian.

But was that strictly true? Just a good time, nothing else?

She knew it wasn't. No matter how much she wished it was no more than a surface, intellectualized affair, she knew it wasn't that shallow. He had gotten past the surface, and not just in the physical sense. He had penetrated in the emotional sense, too. Deeply. And that scared her. Because regardless of the fact that she had been enough in control to be able to send him off to his separate bed last night, she was beginning to realize that her feelings for him were definitely running amok.

* * *

The Colorado Springs Zoo was only moderately crowded on this late September Saturday. The sky was a crisp, flawless blue. A slight autumn breeze mellowed the still-warm temperature, and tall trees deflected the heat of the sun and kept Allyn and Ian from baking as they leisurely followed the paths from exhibit to exhibit.

Oddly enough neither Ian nor Allyn focused primarily on the animals. Ian spent more time watching Allyn, and Allyn spent more time watching the children watching the animals. When she hoisted a toddler up for a better view of the zebras—the second time she had so accommodated the same little boy whose mother was carrying a younger brother—Ian's intent expression broke into a smile.

"You really like kids, don't you?" he said, thinking of her treatment of his nieces, as well.

Allyn shrugged negligently. "Sure. Don't you?"

"Sure, but you seem really drawn to them. For a minute, back there, in the monkey house when you ran after that baby girl as she wandered out I thought you might keep right on going with her."

She looked askance at him. "You think I'm a kidnapper?"

"I just thought you gave her back pretty reluctantly."

"I could use the tax deduction."

"I'm serious."

"I noticed. Zoos are no place to be serious. I thought we came to have a good time."

But he wasn't going to let her off the hook that easily. Now that he thought of it, her response to children struck him as incongruous. Most women who devoted themselves to a career with the intensity she did were not particularly interested in kids. "How long were you married? I don't remember if you've ever said."

"I love the elephants. I'm especially fond of that funny hair that grows along their backs."

Ian tossed peanuts to one of the big gray beasts. "How long?" he persisted.

"Twelve years. You know, a giraffe is an amazing creature. Brit has a face sort of like a giraffe. What did you do with her, anyway?"

"I put her in a kennel for the weekend. Her Airedale stubbornness is too much to thrust on poor Jon. He likes cats." Ian studied Allyn's profile. "Do you realize how bitterly you said 'twelve years'?"

"Must be the echo in here. Lizards and snakes. Yuck."

"Now that I think of it, you always do that, don't you?"

"What? Squirm at the sight of lizards and snakes? Let's go see the penguins."

"Every time I ask about your past, your marriage, you try to avoid answering. If you can't, you give me a glib answer then change the subject yourself. How come?"

She forced a shelled nut into his mouth, widening her eyes and answering like Vincent Price. "Because it's boring with a capital *B*."

He swallowed the peanut and wrapped an arm around her neck, pulling her face in close to his. "If you like kids so much and you were married for twelve years—a long time—why no kids?"

"You are a nosy man, Reed."

"And you're an evasive woman." He grew very solemn as a thought struck. "Did you have kids and lose custody?"

Allyn rolled her eyes. "If it's melodrama you want, you aren't going to find it here. I didn't have any kids. Period. Now, if we don't get moving, we'll miss the last tour through the Cave of the Winds. Stalagmites, stalactites—they even get you deep in the middle of it and turn out the lights so you can experience absolute darkness. Cheat me out of all that and I'll sue for breach of promise," she teased.

"One of these days, I'm going to figure you out," he said, but conceded to her demand and led the way back to the car.

Cave of the Winds was informative if one had a hunger for close encounters with rocks, which both Allyn and Ian agreed afterward they did not. They finished the day with a tour of the Air Force Academy, where they happened upon a wedding in the chapel.

"Weddings," was Allyn's odd comment, "are pagan rites I will never understand. You dress up in costumes and play royalty for a day. There's really something warped about that."

"I suppose you eloped," he teased her.

"No, I did the whole thing. A Cecil B. deMille production. I felt like I was wearing someone else's clothes and cried—all the way down the aisle, all through the service, all through the receiving line. My nose ran, my face puffed and I was more embarrassed than at any other point in my entire life." Then she finished to herself, "Guess I should have taken it as an indication."

"An indication of what?"

She hedged. "Nothing. It's just that I was an unlikely bride. I didn't fit the part."

"Meaning that you didn't fit the part of a wife, either?"

Allyn shrugged. "Guess not. I was unseated, wasn't I?" This time it was she who led the way back to the car.

With the dinner and entertainment choices left up to Allyn that night, they dined on chili dogs and went to the movies. Afterward, when Ian suggested drinks and dancing, Allyn declined in favor of a walk.

Set against Pike's Peak, the Clarion's grounds were landscaped with a touch of the mountains. Aspen trees clustered around artfully pyramided boulders, and a small brook wound like a mountain stream through lush lawns and patches of late-blooming wildflowers.

As they strolled the path that followed the side of the brook Ian took Allyn's hand. "Why do I get the feeling that as hard as I'm trying to show you an extravagant evening, you are determined to keep it ordinary?"

"I don't have to be determined. I'm an ordinary kind of person."

"Then there was a point to this tonight."

"Not consciously," she lied. "You asked what I wanted to do, and I told you."

Ian sighed elaborately, pulled her in close to his side, his elbow in the crook of hers, their entwined hands resting against his chest. "I think there's an ulterior motive."

"Like what?"

"Like: I am what I am, and don't expect me to be anything else."

Caught in the act. "Or maybe I just felt like chili dogs, movies and a walk," she bluffed, pretending an intense interest in the clear, starry sky.

Ian's glance stayed on her for a moment. He sensed that there was so much more beneath her surface. When he spoke again his voice was sincere. "I like you the way you are, and I don't expect you to be anything else."

"Then don't complain about the chili dogs," she teased in response. Hoping he would drop it, she inhaled a deep breath of the cool night air, fragrant with the scent of grass and flowers. "No matter how you look at it, this is nice. I'd like to lie snuggled in a warm bed with all the windows open so I could hear the sound of that stream, smell the smell of fall and feel this cool air on my cheeks."

Ian chuckled slightly, giving in to the scene she painted. "Sounds good to me. Maybe later?"

"Mmm" was all the commitment he was going to get out of her.

They walked in companionable silence, his thumb tracing circles around her knuckles. For a while they were content with silence. Then Ian remembered what he had been meaning to tell her since Thursday.

"Emma is coming home tomorrow. I talked to her Thursday morning. She's miserable. I guess my idea about her getting away was not a good one, so I convinced her to come home."

"Poor Emma. I feel so rotten for her."

"She was also worried about you."

"Me? Why?"

Ian led the way off the path to a cluster of large boulders, finding a spot where he could sit. He pulled Allyn to stand between his spread legs, keeping her prisoner with his arms over her shoulders, his hands locked behind her head. "She said something about September being a bad month for you last year."

"She did? Isn't that odd?" And then, predictably, she changed the subject. "Jon seemed awfully interested every time Emma's name was mentioned as we worked yesterday."

Ian only laughed. It was becoming interesting to see how many different ways she could avoid revealing anything about herself. "Jon has been in love with Emma for years. He was a good friend to Mike. But now... well, now he anticipates a second chance coming his way."

"I see," she said a bit frigidly, feeling defensive for the man who had agreed with his wife and befriended Allyn when she most needed it.

"I think it's great for both Emma and Jon. Emma cares for him; she always has. Once she gets through the grief and is ready, she has only to open her eyes and there he'll be, waiting to take care of her."

Allyn laughed wryly. "Does she need to be taken care of?"

"Maybe she doesn't *need* it, no. But isn't it nice to be taken care of, to have someone to care for in return?"

She thought about that. "I guess it's a matter of preference. I prefer taking care of myself. Realistically, we can all only rely on ourselves."

"Self-reliance is a good thing," he agreed conversationally. "Unless the purpose for it is self-protection. Then it's sad."

"I don't think it's sad. We all need to protect ourselves, too." She looked away from him, watching the lazy flow of the stream.

"From what?"

"A lot of things. Pain and disappointment."

"Not possible. There is no protection from pain and disappointment. They're part of life."

"True, but some of the causes can be avoided."

"Is love one of the causes?"

"Sometimes." And she wasn't doing too well at avoiding that anymore. "You know you really are a sexist to think Emma should be glad to have a man waiting in the wings to take care of her."

"I don't think sexism has anything to do with it. I'm glad she has someone who cares about her." He fluffed Allyn's curly hair with the tip of his nose as she continued to stare at the meandering brook. "I'd like to take care of you, but not out of sexism or necessity. It's out of the feelings I have for you."

The sound of his voice, the feel of his warmth around her, stirred her senses. It had been nice just walking in companionable silence before, enjoying the night. She didn't want to argue sexism. She didn't want to argue anything at all. She just wanted to enjoy being relaxed, unhurried, feeling as lazy as that stream. So she made light of it. "There is one thing I'll let you take care of."

"Name it."

"It even qualifies as extravagant."

"That's what I'm here for."

"I'd love a cup of Spanish coffee."

"Thank goodness." He pushed up from the rock, wrapping one arm around her shoulders to keep her close. "I'm freezing out here and after chili dogs and a Molly Ringwald movie I was afraid I was going to get stuck gagging down a cup of hot chocolate as a nightcap." As they headed back to the hotel, Ian growled facetiously in her ear. "Not that I don't really enjoy hot dogs and Molly Ringwald."

Room service provided Spanish coffee for Allyn and Irish coffee for Ian. The rich concoctions warmed them both and nicely relaxed Allyn. When they had finished, they curled up together on the plump sofa. Tonight, when one kiss led to another and desire grew naturally, Allyn, no longer feeling the need to prove she could control the situation, let it run its course.

It was Ian's bed they shared as their hands and mouths explored, excited and pleasured. Dimly lit by a single bedside lamp, Ian watched every movement, every inch of her exquisite, petite body, as aroused by the sight of her as the feel of her. His fingers combed through the silken curls so close to her head, his tongue traced the sensitive inside of her ear.

"I love you, Allyn," he whispered as his mouth lowered to her breast.

She arched her back to his seeking hand, to his suckling mouth. Her palms rode the muscles of his back and then drew around to his pectorals, teasing his taut male nibs. She tormented him with kisses and tiny bites along the sharp ridge of his collarbone. She reveled in his every touch, returning in kind. But she could not return his words.

Their passion grew frenzied and frantic, exploding in unison and then easing, ebbing, slowly, until their breathing calmed, their racing pulses steadied.

In the comfort of Ian's arms, her head cradled in the hollow of his shoulder, Allyn slept. Ian held her close, one hand stroking gently over the dampness of her hair as the other pulled the sheet up over their sated bodies. Tucking his chin he peered down at her, feeling his love for her like a balloon expanding in his chest, growing greater and stronger with every passing minute.

But she had not said she loved him. She had never said his first name.

And it all felt somehow like a rejection.

Chapter Nine

Allyn fidgeted. She had not been able to sit still through the Sunday-morning drive from Colorado Springs to Denver, and she was no more relaxed as Ian drove to the church for the baptism that afternoon. It struck him as curious.

"Tell me about your family," he coaxed, hoping for a clue.

Allyn pinched one of her own bright red hairs off her corduroy slacks and put it out the window. "Three brothers and a sister, one brother-in-law, one sister-in-law, two nieces, a mother and a father," she accounted.

"A tally tells me nothing," he complained. "Are you close to them?"

"You sound so dubious. As a matter of fact, I am."

He removed his left arm from resting out the window to take control of the steering wheel while he reached his right across the back of the seat and clasped the nape of Allyn's neck. He could feel the cords of tension there. "You seem awfully nervous about this. I thought maybe you didn't get along with them. It isn't having me along, is it?"

She smiled at that. Actually, she was glad he was with her. His presence made this easier, and not just in deflecting the constant barrage of concern for her personal life—or her lack of a personal life to be more precise. She was dreading this and it was nice to have him there.

"It must just be the responsibility of being a godmother." She made light of it, and then gave him a rare look at how she actually felt about him. "I'm glad you came today. I enjoyed Colorado Springs and I wasn't ready for the weekend to be over."

He took his eyes off of the road to look at her, his expression warm. "Thank you" was all he said, the simple words rich with genuine pleasure.

The group that attended the church service was small—only Chris, Dennis, the new baby, Allyn's parents and the friend who would serve as godfather. Dennis's family lived out of state and had not seen fit to make the trip since neither of his sisters had been asked to be godmother, and the rest of the Danner family would come to the house afterward.

Allyn was grateful that Chris held the baby throughout the ceremony and she had only to stand beside her and say her part with the godfather, a tall thin man Dennis had introduced as Jerry. She glanced at the blanketed bundle that was her new niece only if it seemed unavoidable, intense discomfort keeping her stiff, her voice soft.

From the front pew Ian watched the scene. Dennis was the picture of a proud father. Tall and ruddy complexioned, his eyes misted more than once. Chris was of interest to Ian in her difference from Allyn. She was taller and understandably heavier, but there was more to it than appearance. Chris seemed open and relaxed, more comfortable and accepting of herself than Allyn. She smiled easily, laughed just as easily and had a mother-earth air about her. Ian thought she was probably a good mother, patient and likely to get right into the blow-up swimming pool and splash around with her kids.

The elder Danners were handsome people. Bill Danner was tall and thin, young looking in spite of his nearly white cap of curls—obviously from whence Allyn's had come. Marleen Danner was much shorter, slightly smaller than her daughter. She was a compact, chic-looking woman, her blond hair precisely styled, her body trim. Her posture was straight and strong, giving a message of confidence. Ian wondered why it was that Marleen seemed more intent on watching Allyn than the service or her newest grandchild.

Allyn was quiet on the drive from the church to Chris and Dennis's trilevel house in the suburbs. Still tense, she sat stiffly, her features appearing grim above the high white collar of her blouse. Ian wanted to say *Confide in me, let me help*, but realized it was futile and opted for letting her mull over whatever it was that bothered her.

Several cars already lined the street in front of the half-red-brick, half-white-siding house. The door was open and the sound of voices and loud rock music greeted Allyn and Ian through the screen. Without knocking or ringing the bell, Allyn led the way into the plain foyer and then the living room. Scattered on the beige carpeted floor were a doll, a baby blanket and a pair of little pink underpants. Allyn bent to retrieve all three, hiding the underpants in the blanket.

The only person in the living room was the youngest of Allyn's three brothers. Josh barely nodded when he was introduced to Ian, intent on a David Bowie video blaring from the television.

"You'll have to excuse him, he's seventeen," Allyn said to Ian. But it was a sisterly chastisement aimed at her brother at the same time.

Ian only smiled his understanding and followed her through the dining room in the direction of the voices coming from the back of the house.

The Danner family stood clustered in the kitchen, leaning against the oak cupboards or jockeying for position around a platter of vegetables and a bowl of dip that sat in the center of the table. All eyes came their way as Allyn and Ian crossed through the arched doorway from the dining room. Before Allyn could make a full round of introductions, Mitch, the eldest of the Danner children and a replica of his father, promptly held out his hand to Ian and offered him a beer. "We're not fancy around here, I'll show you where the refrigerator is and you can help yourself."

With a bottle of beer in hand, Ian turned back to Allyn where her third brother, Tim, had her in a headlock and was roughing up her hair as if she were one of the boys. Allyn brought an end to that with a vicious tickling of his side and, still held tightly by her brother's arm, her own around his waist, introduced the two men.

Dressed in shorts that exposed thighs like tree trunks, and a polo shirt that cupped every inch of his well-formed torso, Tim was obviously the athlete of the family. "Where's Janet?" he asked as soon as the formalities were over. "We have a bet on this guy. She didn't believe me when I told her Al was bringing a man today. Said I was nuts, that Al was a confirmed single person. I have five bucks on you."

Janet came from across the kitchen. She was a tall, lissome blonde who hung on to her husband's free arm as if he might escape.

"Five bucks. Pay up," Tim demanded when he had concluded the introduction.

She only smiled contentedly and cooed, "Take it out in trade."

"They've only been married for a few months," Allyn said by way of explanation as Tim growled his agreement and planted a sloppy, openmouthed kiss on his wife. Allyn disengaged herself from her brother's other arm and led Ian to the buffet table.

Within the atmosphere of friendliness Ian was made to feel like one of the family almost instantly. Marleen made sure his plate was filled, while in line in front of him Bill kept up a running joke about all the food the women would force him to eat as he piled his own plate high. Mitch, who was a corporate lawyer, talked business. Tim, who ran a health club, talked sports, and Josh, who pried himself away from his videos only for food, was particularly interested in Ian's Rolex watch and Mercedes sports car parked out front. Dennis pointed out the raspberry bushes—his particular pride and joy—that grew just beyond the patio where they all gathered to eat. Chris teased him about wearing a suit and didn't give up until she had divested him of coat and tie and persuaded him to roll his sleeves up to his elbows, and even Janet managed a few intelligent questions from where she perched on Tim's lap.

Within the close atmosphere, Allyn relaxed somewhat. She sat beside Ian at the picnic table with her own plate of food and laughed when she found a spot of barbecue sauce on the tip of his nose. When he'd missed it himself for the third time she even wiped it off for him.

When they had all eaten, Dennis finished taking movies on his newest acquisition, a videocassette camera. Passed around like a rag doll, once the filming was over, tiny Holly Patterson was finally put to bed in her cradle upstairs. Her two-year-old sister Ashley lasted only a little while longer. Helped by her Uncle Tim to reach the folding table that held coffee, nuts, candy and cake, Ashley finger-painted through the blue 'God Bless Holly' frosting writing, stuffed a full five mints into her mouth at once and dribbled pink and green saliva down the front of her white dress. Taking her from Tim, it was her Uncle Mitch who stoically washed her hands and face in the kitchen sink and then bribed her with a piggyback ride to bed for a nap.

Once the kids were tucked away and the plates and buffet table cleaned, the adults gathered in the family room downstairs to watch Dennis's movies on the videocassette player.

"If you would rather, we can duck out now," Allyn offered Ian, herself not enthusiastic about watching old home movies recently transferred to videotape.

Ian gave her a genuine smile. "Believe it or not, I'm looking forward to it."

Allyn sat through about fifteen minutes of the first film of Ashley's baptism two years ago. Two years ago. Everyone was there to celebrate the new baby, the first grandchild. Everyone but Allyn.

A sharp memory struck her so hard it nearly took her breath away. She remembered only too well the hospital bed in which she'd been that very same day. She remembered only too well what she had been feeling.

She couldn't watch.

Allyn silently snuck out.

The kitchen sink was cluttered with the small plates, cups and saucers left from dessert. Glad for an excuse to busy herself, she cleaned up the mess. The sounds of the oohs and ahs of her family could be heard even over the running water, and she knew, without having to see the movies, that the subject matter was Ashley's infancy.

Her stomach knotted.

She turned the water up higher, hoping to drown out the sound.

Chris's kitchen was a cheery place done in red and white. Her sister kept it in an organized clutter of useable items and knickknacks that formed no particular style—just Chris's style. There were duck-head hooks for towels, copper pots, old-fashioned cans for canisters, an ultramodern coffeepot, a plain whistler tea kettle. A Jenny Lind high chair took a place at the Early American kitchen table, and oatmeal had dried on the edges of both the tray and the table. Allyn scrubbed it until she got it off.

Anything to keep busy.

Anything to keep herself from going upstairs.

She washed and dried the glass coffeepot, replaced the sugar bowl in the cupboard and took the milk that had been used as coffee cream to put back into the refrigerator.

The refrigerator door was a collage of receipts, cartoons, notes of reminder, finger paintings and crayon scribbling held in place with magnets that looked like hamburgers, pizza slices, ice-cream bars and puffy old women's faces made out of nylon stockings.

Allyn put the milk in the refrigerator, and when she closed the door, one of the overburdened magnets came loose and several photographs fell to the floor.

They were pictures of Holly, Allyn couldn't help but notice as she picked them up. Holly having her first bath. Holly being awkwardly held by Ashley. Holly looking like she was about to scream bloody murder. Holly nestled into her mother's shoulder, all the sweetness of the back of her neck captured by the camera....

Allyn's stomach knotted even tighter.

She hastily replaced the photos and swung away from the sight to search for something else to do. But the kitchen was clean now. There was no more excuse to stay there.

And that baby was all alone in her nursery upstairs.

Josh was back in the living room watching MTV so Allyn decided to try that. He smiled at her when she came in, but that was as far as the interruption to his attention went. The next second, his eyes were pinched shut, his lips were curled back in a grimace that under any other circumstances would have appeared to be agony, his shoulders were hunched sharply forward and he was playing a mean air guitar.

Allyn laughed to herself and made a mental note of the song and performers to get him the album for his birthday in two weeks.

It was then that she heard the baby cry from upstairs.

Her throat constricted as she waited for it to stop. Or for someone else to hear.

But Josh was engrossed in his imaginary accompaniment and everyone else was laughing loudly at Dennis's home movies in the lower-floor family room.

Maybe Holly would go back to sleep.

Allyn swallowed hard and plunged her hands into her pants pockets as if that tied her up, too.

But the baby only cried harder.

"Take care of her, will you, Al?" Josh said without opening his eyes. "I don't know about babies."

She has a mother, Allyn wanted to say but didn't, working to push back the panic-induced harshness. For a moment she considered slipping back into the family room and announcing that Holly was crying, but she discounted the idea. There had already been comments—didn't she want to hold her goddaughter at least once? Allyn knew that the positive effect of bringing Ian would be negated by her obvious anxiety, making everyone start worrying about her again.

As if she were about to face a firing squad, Allyn climbed the four steps up to the bedrooms.

The nursery was decorated with teddy bears and balloons, darkened by a curtain that matched the wallpaper. In the cradle the tiny infant was red-faced with outrage, squalling in that grating way newborns do. For a moment Allyn only stood peering down at her niece, willing her to stop on her own...before she had to touch her.

But the baby didn't stop. She kept right on crying.

Slowly Allyn drew her hands from her pockets and reached for Holly. She lifted her awkwardly, at first reluctant to snuggle the baby against her body. But then she did, holding her close. The instant Holly was settled in the soft warmth of her aunt's arms she stopped crying. *She's a cuddler* Chris had said. *She just likes to be held.*

The tiny infant rooted, her clenched fist accidentally brushed her own round cheek and she greedily turned toward it and sucked for all she was worth, making sloppy sounds. Her eyes never opened, but the redness went out of her face and contentment smoothed her brow.

Allyn closed her own eyes and rubbed her cheek against the downy softness of Holly's head. Back and forth. Back and forth.

And then it was Allyn who cried.

Standing silently in the doorway to the nursery, Ian watched it all. He had come to find Allyn just as she climbed the stairs to the bedrooms and followed her. Over the baby's squalls she hadn't heard him say her name, and then his curiosity had been aroused by her reaction to the infant, and he had watched rather than pressing the point of his presence.

At first he had thought it just a normal response, similar to her fond reaction to the kids at the zoo. But the longer she held her niece, the less ordinary it seemed. It was when she bent her cheek to the baby's head and began to sway with her that he saw the tears.

The sight of Allyn holding that baby, her body wrapped around her as if she would absorb it if she could, tears coursing down her face, wrenched Ian's insides. He wanted to go to her, hold her as protectively as she held Holly, do anything he could to comfort her. But he knew her well enough to realize she would only get angry at any intrusion. She would be embarrassed, and to hide that, she would lash out. So instead he reluctantly left her to herself, troubled by what he had seen.

Back in the family room Ian's reentrance caught the attention of Chris. She flashed him a warm smile, but he could only frown at her in return. Taken aback, Chris left her spot on the couch and came to him.

"Something wrong?" she whispered so no one else in the room could hear.

"Can we talk?" he answered, equally as quietly.

Chris curled her arm through his and took him up to the kitchen. "What's the matter?" she asked, when they had both taken chairs at the table, her smile showing her own confidence that nothing too bad could have happened.

Ian nodded in the direction of the upstairs bedrooms. "Allyn is in the nursery crying over your new baby," he said bluntly, watching for Chris's reaction.

Her expression sobered. She took a deep breath. "Oh" was all she said.

"You don't find that odd or startling," he observed.

She stood and fiddled with a dish towel that was caught half out of a cupboard door. Ian thought, *the whole damn family is good at evasion,* but he merely waited.

"I don't know much about your relationship with Allyn," Chris finally said, obviously testing before saying too much.

"I'm in love with her," he admitted blatantly, hoping it might help.

Slightly startled, Chris nevertheless maintained her composure. "I see. How does she feel?"

"Your guess is as good as mine. I may be wrong, but I think I'm the only man that's gotten this far into her life since her divorce. She's fighting it like hell, but I believe she cares about me, and I can tell you for sure that I'm in for the long haul."

Chris dried out the sink, never looking his way. "Has she told you about her divorce?"

"Only that it was just a parting. She made it sound amiable, but I'm beginning to wonder."

"It was definitely not amiable." The words slipped out in a tone of heavy sarcasm. "But she hasn't told you anything else?"

Ian admitted only reluctantly, "Nothing."

"Then I don't think I should."

"For crying out loud, Chris, was it so bad that it has to be a national secret?"

She turned to face him then, leaning back against the counter, her arms crossed. "Divorce can be traumatic. I know that might seem dated these days when it happens so often. The contemporary attitude is often out with the old, on to the new, mutual decisions by consenting adults, equal division, no hard feelings. But the truth of it is that even now, divorce isn't always by mutual agreement, and even perfectly contemporary people get badly hurt. Some get traumatized. Allyn had a bad time of it."

"I only want to help her."

"I don't doubt that. But if she had wanted you to know she would have told you. I certainly can't tell what she wouldn't. It isn't my place."

Ian stood and pushed his chair in to the table, his expression solemn but determined. "Then I guess it's time I take off the kid gloves."

He went upstairs, Chris following close behind. "I'm not so sure that's a good idea. Allyn comes to things in her own way, at her own pace. She always has. Maybe patience is a better idea."

But Ian only shook his head and gently pushed open the nursery door.

The curtains were still pulled, keeping the room dim. The teddy bears still floated from the ends of balloon strings among cottony clouds. Holly slept peacefully in her cradle.

But Allyn was nowhere around.

For a few minutes after Dennis let him off in front of Emma's garage, Ian just stood looking up at the apartment. The Mercedes was parked in its usual spot, the keys in the ignition—just as they had been at Dennis and Chris's house when Allyn had quietly walked out and driven herself home.

If he hadn't realized that he loved her before, he surely would have as he stood here, torn apart by the thought of her being all alone with a pain he didn't understand.

Ian climbed the steps to Allyn's front door.

She didn't answer his knock. But he hadn't expected her to. He used the key that was on the ring Emma had left him.

Allyn sat on the daybed like a wilted flower, but the expression that greeted Ian was disgusted. "If I had wanted company I would have let you in myself."

Ignoring her words, Ian closed the door and sat beside her, careful not to touch her even though he was aching to. "And if I'd wanted to be stranded today I would have picked a tropical island," he said.

Allyn let her head drop back, rolling it around. A popping sound filled the silence, announcing the tension that had tightened her neck. "Sorry about the car. But you seem to have gotten home all right, and I didn't wreck it, so all's well that ends well." She should have told him to leave, she knew. There would be questions if he stayed. She had left Chris's house to be alone . . . had *needed* to be alone then. But here he was, and for some reason that she didn't understand, just his presence seemed to help. She was too wrung out to analyze it.

"I don't think this ended too well," Ian said gently.

"Strange day."

"For you. I'd like to know why."

Allyn sighed and pushed herself up from the daybed. "I'd like a glass of wine. Would you?"

More evasion. Ian gave in to it and followed her into the kitchen half of the open apartment. "I'll get the Styrofoam cups."

For a while after the wine had been poured, Allyn stood leaning against the counter, her glass in hand, staring at a spot on the floor. She sucked her bottom lip in, ruminating as if she didn't have company at all.

Ian watched and waited. "I'd like to know what's going on in your head."

"I know you would." She straightened from the counter and went back to the daybed, this time sitting on the floor. With her back against it, she pulled her bent knees in close to her chest and used them as a brace for her forearm, her cup lightly tapping into her thigh in a slow rhythm.

Ian sat on the coffee table, facing her at a right angle, his legs spread, his elbows resting on them, his own wine ignored as he continued to watch her. "Will you tell me?"

She thought about that. In the past two years she had avoided rehashing what had happened in her life. There was a simple enough reason for it—it had been ugly and painful and talking about it stirred memories of that pain. But today she was hurting anyway. So, why not?

"It's a cliché," she warned.

"I won't take off points for lack of originality." God, how he wanted to hold her, just to touch her. But she seemed so self-protective, so carefully balanced, he didn't dare.

"High-school sweethearts marry at eighteen," she said as if reading a headline. "Husband and wife work toward one goal—husband's education, husband's career."

"Why don't you leave out the sarcasm and just tell me what happened," he suggested compassionately.

Allyn's smile was ironic. "I'm not sure I can do that. Melodrama or sarcasm, there doesn't seem to be another way for me to get it into words."

"Try."

She took a deep breath, and when she spoke again her voice was normal, if a bit distant. "When I was eighteen I married a man named Keith O'Neal. A nice guy, that was Keith. Everybody liked him. Everybody could count on him. Sensitive, caring, considerate, compassionate...." Her voice dwindled off, and then she laughed a facetious little laugh as her mind wandered for a moment.

Then she went on. "Once we were married I thought that investing in him was what I was supposed to do. I thought that investing in his education, in his goals, in his future, was the same as investing in my own. I know, it's an old-fashioned, prefeminist idea, but that's what I was raised around. My parents got married right out of high school and stayed together, my grandparents stayed with it right up to the death-do-we-part stuff. Divorce just wasn't something commonplace in my family, it wasn't something you protected yourself against. That would have been a negative attitude. You got married, and together you both worked for the future. Period. Naive, but . . . well, that's how I thought. And after all, Keith was a great guy. No one doubted the wisdom of trusting him, certainly not me.''

She sipped her wine and sighed, seeming more relaxed now that she had gotten into it.

''So Keith went to school, got a bachelor's degree in marketing, then a master's in business, and then he went to work for Husby Oil at the height of the oil boom. And he made a splash. The man was good, intelligent, talented, ambitious, attractive. . . . And I was a great support system, even if I do say so myself. He talked my ears off about every little detail in his job, asked my advice, took it more often than not, gave me strokes for my insights and wisdom . . . we were a team. I thought. Anyway, he started the ascent up the corporate ladder, boosted with accolades from his supervisors and strokes to his ego. He made friends and contacts. He became very popular in the business community. . . . Let us not forget that he was such a nice guy. . . .

''At any rate, we had a lot of debts but there was light at the end of the tunnel. Years of doing without were going to pay off. We were going to start a family.''

Ian watched her sober remarkably. It didn't take a genius to know this was still a raw nerve. He waited for her to go on, but when she seemed stuck he prompted with a guess. ''Does this have anything to do with September?''

''Ah, yes, September,'' Allyn confirmed. ''September twentieth to be exact. His birthday. Our twelfth anniversary. He had just gotten a really big promotion and raise. I decided on a splurge to celebrate all three. I went out and bought him a stereo system—one of those massive, expensive, high-tech things. It was going to be a big surprise. I had it delivered that day and set up. I was so excited...." Again, the harsh little laugh. "He really liked it, too. Just what he wanted." Allyn looked Ian in the eye. "He said he and the woman he loved would enjoy it. Funny thing, though, I wasn't that woman."

"Oh, no, Allyn."

"Oh, yes. Guess his surprise topped mine. As he explained it to me, he had become the perfect Yuppie— whatever that means. And I was just the uneducated hausfrau who didn't fit in with his new image, his new friends, his new interests. I was holding him back. Personally, I think his ego dwarfed his brain, but maybe that's jaded." She shook her head and spoke almost in an aside for a moment. "It's a frightening thing to realize how dependent you are on someone else. That another person can control what happens to you, can suddenly take away everything you worked for."

Then she went on with her story. "He had become obsessed with his career, with himself actually, but I accepted it as part of the package, never guessing. She— the Other Woman—was his twenty-two-year-old assistant. Working together they had grown closer and closer, he said. She was the best, and he deserved the best." Her voice grew quiet. "I don't know what that made me. The worst, I guess." She shook her head sadly.

"He packed up and took the things he wanted—besides the stereo—the few things he thought were good enough for him and his new life, and left me like an old, chipped table he didn't need anymore. I had half the debts and none of the future, and there wasn't a thing I could do about it." She swallowed, took a deep breath and said, "And then I found out I was pregnant." She toasted the air. "Here's to you, Keith O'Neal."

As she took a drink of her wine, Ian tried to absorb that last bombshell. "What happened to the baby?" he asked very, very softly.

She answered almost as softly. "After he told me all of this and left, the pain and hatred I felt were like the world's biggest Roman candle inside of me—hot, sharp sparks. There didn't seem to be any outlet, any way to put the Roman candle out, to even cap it off. I was in a daze, stunned, out of sync with everything, incapable of even thinking straight. I couldn't eat. I couldn't sleep. Even my reflexes were off kilter. I was treacherous behind the wheel of a car...."

"The baby?" he prompted softly, thinking she was rambling.

"I had two fender benders—nothing serious, but it should have been enough for me to hang up my keys until things settled down. I just didn't realize how out of touch I was. There was a third accident. More than a fender bender. I hit a parked car—luckily no one was in it at the time. But for me...well, poor nutrition, little rest, Roman candles for emotions, tension that made me feel like the top of my head was going to blow off and then a car accident..." She closed her eyes, swallowing back tears convulsively. Her voice cracked with emotion. "I lost the baby."

"I'm so sorry, Allyn," was all he could say.

It took a moment of struggling with her own grief, of fighting the tears she was too proud to shed openly. But when she had conquered them both she managed a sad smile. "Me, too." But then she drew a deep breath, raised her eyebrows and seemed to relax, as if the telling had been a release. "Anyway, as much as I wanted that baby, at least there didn't end up being a child Keith could hurt, too. And without the baby the ties could be completely severed. I was grateful for that."

A concern of his own cropped up, and Ian couldn't keep from asking. "How do you feel about the man now?"

Allyn laughed easily enough and answered without hesitation. "Keith O'Neal is a powerless piece of the past."

"But what came out of it is a pretty powerful need to succeed. Are you sure you aren't trying to prove something to him?"

"Positive. What came out of it was not so much a need to succeed as a good lesson on a woman's need to be self-sufficient, self-reliant and keep all her eggs in her own basket. Not to relinquish control of her life," she said without rancor. "So there you have it. The story of my life: What Makes Allyn Run."

"And today I saw what made Allyn cry."

She sobered once more. "That's what you get for spying," she grumbled, embarrassed.

"The marriage and the man may be old news, but the baby is still an open wound."

She tried to shrug it away. "We all have soft spots."

"Not as soft as what I saw today. I would expect a person who wants a baby as badly as you do to be putting as much time into her personal life as she is into her professional." Then something else struck him and he asked softly, "Or did the miscarriage leave you incapable?"

"I was assured that there was no damage done."

"Then answer the first part."

"Guess I've just gone on to other things," she said glibly. Standing all of a sudden, she took both of their cups to toss in the trash.

Ian recognized the invitation to leave and the evasion in it. He ignored it and challenged instead. "Now try the truth."

"That's the truth. I've bared my soul to you today, why would I stop now?"

"Because this is where I come in."

"Excuse me?"

"Everything you've talked about has been in the past. But I'm the threat of a personal life in the present, of getting involved with another man. So you don't want to talk about it. I think the truth is that even as desperately as you want to have kids you're more afraid of being hurt again. Painful as it is to see other people's children, to be near your sister's babies, you choose to suffer that rather than take another chance on loving a man. On loving me."

"You have it all figured out," she said snidely.

"Deny it."

"I don't have to deny anything. You can think what you like."

"I'm thinking it, alright, but I don't like it at all. Give yourself a chance to be happy, for God's sake—to have what you want."

"That's exactly what I'm doing with Danner's Decadent Desserts."

"And what about wanting babies?"

"We can't always have everything we want. I learned that lesson, too."

"But this is something you can have if only you'll take the chance for it."

"Never again," she shouted finally, in frustration and fear of being tempted to think just that. "I promised myself that I would never, never again be that wrapped up in a man or let any man be the core of my life. Taking a chance on loving again is something I refuse to do. Now will you get out of here so I can mix doughs for tomorrow and have a little peace and quiet?"

Ian had come up against too many brick walls in negotiations not to recognize one when he hit it. She was adamant. She had good reason to be adamant. But he had also learned that sometimes patience and gentle persuasion could wear down brick wall adamance that bulldozing couldn't budge. He backed off, standing to leave as she had asked. But before he went out the door he turned back to her.

"Too late" was all he said.

Nothing more needed to be said. They both knew she was already loving again.

Chapter Ten

Monday morning found Ian waiting at the gates of Continental Airlines rather than helping Allyn. Emma had called at midnight on Sunday to explain why she was still in Boston and not on her way home. The twins were having a particularly difficult time adjusting to school after the trauma of their father's death. Both girls were suffering sleeping problems. Elizabeth had severe insomnia, and while Ann could fall asleep, nightmares awakened her after only a few hours. Emma was trying to decide whether it would be better to force them to stay and wait out this adjustment period, or to bring them home with her.

When the twins followed their mother off the plane Ian was not surprised. He wrapped an arm around each of their shoulders, pulled them in close and kissed their temples in turn. Both girls perked up at the attention, giggling, squirming and hanging on tight—so tight that he kept hold of them and only craned his neck forward to kiss Emma hello.

"Now, this is heaven," he teased, squeezing his nieces. "Three women all to myself. What more could a man want?"

"Not a house to himself, I hope," Emma countered.

"How's Brit?" Elizabeth asked anxiously.

"Loud as ever. Does that dog ever stop barking?"

"You didn't let her, did you?" Ann's eyes were wide with concern. "Bud calls the dogcatcher if she barks too much."

"I do what I'm told. I left her in the house when I was gone and never let her stay outside if she was on one of her jags—which is most of the time. No wonder the neighbors complain."

"It's the squirrels' fault; that's what she barks at," Elizabeth said, defending their pet, then grumbled, "Bud needs earplugs, is all."

"What about Allyn?" Ann chimed in. "Did she know we were coming home?"

Ian shook his head. "I told her I couldn't work with her today because I was picking up your mother, but even I didn't know about you two turkeys coming home."

"Turkeys?" they shouted in unison.

"You're the turkey," Elizabeth rejoined.

"Yeah," Ann put in gleefully. "You're such a turkey, Grandma should have named you Tom. Then you'd be Uncle Tom the Turkey."

"Would you teach your daughters to have respect for their elders?"

But Emma's eyebrows rose at something else entirely. "You're working with Allyn?"

Ian grinned at his sister. "There isn't any other way to spend time with her, is there?"

"What do you do with Allyn?" Ann interrupted excitedly.

"Yes, what *do* you do with Allyn, Ian?" Emma taunted curiously.

"Oh, I grease pans, stir dough, burn myself, break glass, help with deliveries—nothing too hard."

"Uncle Ian is Allyn's assistant," Elizabeth said in singsong.

"I thought you came to work at a bank this time." Ann was confused.

"I think he has a crush on Allyn." Elizabeth was the more intuitive of the two.

"You do?" Ann's eyes widened.

"The question is, does Allyn have a crush on Uncle Ian?" Emma asked of her brother.

"Uncle Ian hopes so," he mouthed over the girls' heads. But to them he said, "Too late, I'm already in love with you two. If she wants me, she's out of luck. Shall we go see if your luggage is in yet so you turkeys can get home to that mangy mutt of yours?"

"She isn't mangy," squealed Elizabeth.

"Takes a turkey to know a turkey," taunted Ann.

With his arms still holding them tightly, Ian led the way to the baggage claim.

"What's up, little brother?" Emma came up from behind Ian as he sat on the bricked patio watching the garage apartment late that afternoon. She reached a glass of iced tea over his shoulder, resting her hand there when he had taken it.

"You're getting sneaky in your old age, Em. I didn't hear you coming. Feel better being home?" he asked, instead of answering.

"Mmm. As good as anything feels right now, I guess." Emma pulled a lounger beside his chair and sat down, bracing her own tea on the arm.

"What made you decide to bring the girls back with you?"

"Oh, I know it probably doesn't seem smart," she said defensively. "The school psychologist said I should give it more time—ten days wasn't enough. But things have been bad enough for them lately. For us all, for that matter. I needed them. They needed me. If it's spoiling them, so what, I'll spoil them. That psychiatrist can go to hell."

Ian laughed. "I see a little of Allyn's militancy has rubbed off on you."

Emma laughed, too, and then went on with less fervor. "All of our security is kind of shaken right now. I thought getting back to their friends and school, back to normal, would be better than keeping them here with all the memories, putting them in a new school. But they convinced me they would rather be here in their own home, with Brit and Allyn and you and me."

"Not in that order, I hope."

"No, Allyn comes before Brit this time. She provided shelter from the storm those last awful weeks. I don't think they're done needing that yet." Emma took a sip of her tea just as Elizabeth came bounding out of the house with her tape player in hand.

The wiry girl paused only long enough to pop a kiss on her uncle's cheek before running full speed to her sister, who waited on the tennis court.

Emma watched her daughters. "From the looks of things today, I think you've been elected as stand-in father, I hope you don't mind."

"Mind? Those two little twits are the nicest things that have ever happened to me. I love them, you know that."

Emma's eyes filled, as they so easily did these days. "Thanks," she said brokenly. "It means a lot to me that you feel the way you do about them, that you treat them the way you do and they have you to play daddy for them. Little girls need that, you know. They practice being women on their fathers."

Ian reached over and squeezed his sister's face, half playfully, half lovingly. "What about school?"

Emma swallowed back her tears and seized the change of subject. "There's a private one not far from here. I'm sure I can get them in there without a problem, Mike was instrumental in pulling the financing together when it opened. I'll call tomorrow and get an appointment. I also need to see about some grief counseling. Jon suggested it when I had dinner with him in New York, and I think it's a good idea for us all."

"I agree."

"And how are things coming with Allyn?"

"Things?"

"Mmm. Whatever things caused you to bring Jon to Denver to handle a merger you were supposed to do. Whatever things caused you to become her assistant . . . and her to *let* you become her assistant. Whatever things caused you both to be gone for the entire weekend so that my phone calls all day Saturday and Sunday to both here and her place were never answered."

"Keeping tabs on me, big sister?"

"Just curious."

"And still protective of your tenant?"

"Yes."

Ian drank his tea, his gaze sticking to the garage apartment. "I would hesitate to say this to anyone but a woman who met and married her husband of fifteen years in a mere two weeks, but you should understand. I'm in love with the lady."

Emma sobered once more. "How does she feel?"

He shrugged. "Scared, I think." Ian gave his sister a condensed version of Allyn's past. "I'm the first man she's let past the barriers."

"Pardon my prying, but how far past have you gotten?"

"As far as a weekend away could get me, but not as far as I'd like."

"In bed but not ready to run off to Rio with you," Emma surmised.

"Unfortunately."

"What do you want from her, Ian?"

"Everything. Everything the idiot she was married to had and threw away. I just don't think it's going to be easy for her to give it a second time."

"Understandably."

Sylvia was waiting with a message when Allyn made her deliveries to McCauley's that morning—Carusoe wanted to see her in his office, first thing, the busboys were to unload the van.

Hope sprang to life inside Allyn.

Sylvia was skeptical. "Things aren't good around here, Al, and he's in a foul mood."

But Allyn wouldn't accept a damper. "Then at least I may be safe from that couch he tried to tackle me onto the last time." She headed through the storage room stacked with commercial-size cans and sacks of flour and sugar, calling back over her shoulder to her friend, "If I scream, come running with your rolling pin."

One knock on Carusoe's door brought a bark of entry. The office was a windowless space equipped with more toys than business necessities. A well-stocked bar filled an alcove behind a metal desk, shelves housed a television, video recorder and the stereo system that supplied music to the restaurant. The walls above the gray filing cabinets displayed pennants for the Denver Nuggets Basketball team and the Denver Broncos football team, while on either side were a basketball hoop and a dart board.

Allyn stepped not more than three feet into the room, leaving the miniature pool table and the foosball table separating her from where Carusoe stood rummaging frantically through a file drawer.

"Sylvia said you wanted to see me," Allyn reminded him when he didn't acknowledge her. She hoped that not only did he have news about investors, but that he might pay his bill as well. Carusoe was two months past due, but things being what they were she couldn't risk pressuring him.

Slam! He shoved the drawer closed and turned on her. "Just a minute," he snapped, proceeding to search the trash basket beside his desk.

She merely waited. Sylvia had been right: Carusoe's temper didn't bode well for either matter on which Allyn's hopes were hung.

"Dammit!"

Now it was Carusoe's shout that jarred her. Allyn was intensely uncomfortable. "Maybe it would be better if we talk tomorrow," she suggested.

"There won't be a tomorrow," he snarled without looking at her.

That took her up short. "Excuse me?"

Carusoe found what he was looking for—a small slip of receipt paper—set it carefully on his desk and finally looked at Allyn.

As he spoke he sauntered to the foosball table and gave a dizzying spin to one of the lines of hapless wooden men. "I wanted to see you to cancel any future orders from Danner's Decadent Desserts."

Dumbstruck, Allyn stared at him. "I don't understand. If this has anything to do with this past weekend..."

The Latin man gave a disgusted laugh. "You really think you're something, don't you? I have too many things on my mind to waste time wondering what you do with your weekends. Some jackass with a head cold comes in here to give me a review, spends half an hour sniffling and goes out and ruins me. Business drops, I have to cut back. It's cheaper to do the desserts here, so you're out. That's life."

Allyn shook her head in denial. "If it's only cost, we can work something out. When you find investors and I can expand, business will increase and we can agree on a discount—professional courtesy for your help—that would only be fair. Until then I'm sure we can figure out something."

"Investors?" He nearly spat the word, as if the very thought was a ridiculous fantasy on her part. "Sorry. I didn't have any luck there."

Period? That's it? As if it were just an afterthought? Allyn stared at him, light just beginning to dawn. "You were all talk, weren't you? You just led me on. All of your connections and contacts—that was hype to make you look like a big man, wasn't it?''

"Or maybe you aren't as good as you think, and nobody was interested," he sneered back.

"Did you even try? Or was every bit of it lies?"

His glance ran assessingly up and down her body. "You tease me, I tease you. Look at it that way. Here's a check for what I owe you." He tossed it across the pool table at her.

"You bastard."

He only shrugged and went back to his desk. "I'm a busy man. You want to throw a fit, do it outside."

Allyn let her eyes bore into him a moment longer, all of her contempt and disillusionment reflected there. But she was too furious to even think of anything else to say. She swiped up her check and left.

Allyn finished her day's work on instinct. Her thoughts were in a muddle, her emotions running from rage to fear and back to rage again, all of it shot through with a frustration she knew only too well; the frustration born of feeling powerless, as if everything were out of her control, as if everything she wanted and had planned on had been devastated on someone else's whim.

Ian was waiting for her when she drove around the house that evening. She was not pleased to see him. Long accustomed to licking her wounds in private, she was reluctant to expose them now, even to Ian. But there he waited, at the foot of the wooden steps that led to her outside door.

She forced a weak smile. "I'm rotten company tonight. I think it's better if I just crawl into a hole by myself. I hope you don't mind."

He clasped the nape of her neck and squeezed, his eyebrows dipping together in concern. "Something went wrong?" he guessed.

"I think that qualifies as an understatement." She forced a smile. "I lost the McCauley's account today. And to top it off, I found out that Carusoe was all talk and no action. There were no investors. He probably never even intended to approach anyone on my behalf. So, you can see why my mood is nasty. Run while you can."

"I think I can bear the strain." Ignoring her effort to get rid of him, he climbed the stairs behind her, took her keys, unlocked the door and held it open for her to precede him in.

For some reason the sound of his voice, the sensation of his touch, had a soothing effect that nothing else had all day long. She decided she had enough problems without fighting this, too. "Stay at your own risk then," she warned as she crossed the threshold.

Allyn didn't bother to turn on a light, leaving the only illumination coming from the dusky sky outside. She kicked off her shoes with enough vengeance for them to hit the wall and make black marks. With her arms up over her head in surrender, she fell back onto the day-bed and breathed a colorful, very unladylike expletive.

"Is this as desperate a situation as it looks?" he teased gently as he closed the door.

"'Desperate' is exactly the right term," she admitted, his levity lost on her. "I'm ruined."

He came to sit on the coffee table, facing her, leaning his elbows on his knees. "Does Carusoe really have the power to do that?" Ian returned sensibly.

After a moment of thought she admitted, "I don't know. Only time will tell. Losing the McCauley account is a killer. That's a third of my profits." Allyn shot up and began to pace, agitatedly, angrily. "When will I ever learn?" she ranted. "You'd think I would know better than to depend on someone else for what I need." She hit her palm against her forehead. "Idiot!"

"You took a chance, love. My understanding was that you had exhausted every other possibility and had a basis for believing—or at least hoping—that Carusoe was capable of producing investors. There's nothing foolish about that. Worse risks have been taken."

"But maybe not with as much at stake."

Watching her pace in circles, Ian stood, took her tennis shoes out of the closet and handed them to her. "If you're going to walk we might as well do it out in the fresh air. It'll make you feel better."

Allyn snarled and put on her shoes. Five minutes later she was burning leather down the driveway and then up the street, with Ian easily keeping pace.

They walked for a long while in silence until Ian could tell by her decreasing speed that Allyn was wearing her anger out. Then he offered reason. "As bad as it is to have your hopes dashed and a drop in your business, I think you're losing sight of some other things."

"Such as?" she snapped.

"Such as the fact that you've worked to establish a reputation for quality and reliability. I doubt this will actually put you out of business, will it?"

He was right. Allyn felt marginally better. The frown she angled up at him was too exaggerated to be totally serious. "I'm not looking for sane, rational, reasoning here, Reed. You're supposed to be holding my hand, agreeing with what a creep Carusoe is and feeling sorry for me."

He held her hand. He even patted it compassionately. But his grin said loudly that he refused to take it as seriously as she did. "Carusoe is the worst kind of creep, and I do feel sorry for you. And for me because I waited to eat, figuring I could persuade you to have a late dinner with me. How about at least an ice-cream cone?" He nodded toward The Apple Tree Shanty ice cream and sandwich shop in the shopping center they had inadvertently walked to.

"How can I think of food at a time like this?" she groused overdramatically.

"I could twist your arm," he offered.

"You could have left me to pout in peace."

"In my vast experience with career-women-meeting-obstacles I have found peaceful pouting to be singularly ineffective and ice cream to be the universal cure-all."

"Well, you'll have to buy. I'm nearly unemployed. And I can be a prodigious ice-cream consumer," she threatened, then marched into The Apple Tree Shanty.

Allyn wasn't kidding. She had a triple dip of peanut-butter chocolate fudge. Ian marveled at the most food he had seen her consume at one sitting since they had met. "You must be upset," he observed between bites of his own double dip.

"And you're boring. A double dip of plain chocolate? Didn't your world travels give you a taste for more adventure than that?"

They walked back home at a more relaxed pace, most of the tension gone from Allyn, though the creases that continued to line her forehead were an indication that the early evening's events still worried her. Ian saw it and asked with genuine interest, "What's your next move?"

Allyn shrugged. "I don't really know. Wait and see. Try to drum up more business to fill the gap left by McCauley's—whatever I have to do to make ends meet again. Expansion is out of the question now. I still can't get money through a bank, and I don't have enough connections to find investors of my own. Until the universe presents me with another way, there isn't anything I can do toward that goal."

Once back at her apartment, Ian vetoed her feebly delivered resistance to having his help with preparations for the next day's desserts, again following her upstairs.

Regardless of the fact that they had been intimate on two occasions, Allyn went into the bathroom to change into her dough-mixing clothes. In the confines of the small room her thoughts ran to Ian and the difference in the way she felt at that moment, compared to how she had felt when she'd come home tonight. And overindulgence in ice cream had nothing to do with it.

As reluctant as she had been to see him, she had to admit that without Ian she would probably still be feeling rotten. It had been nice to have someone to share her burden with, someone to help her put things into a less bleak perspective. Nice to have a relationship with a man who was unselfish, who saw her as a person in her own right, who didn't discount her goals, her interests, her worries, as unimportant beside his own.

Somewhere along the way her guard had dropped, she realized.

When had she stopped fighting her feelings about him? Denying them? Stopped looking for faults in him and instead let herself appreciate his good points? But, strangely, it didn't frighten her as it had before. Maybe because, beyond love, she realized she now felt trust.

Trust she thought she would never again feel for any man. But there it was. In full force. For Ian Reed. And in the sunlight of that trust, the seedling of the love that had been a niggling shadow stretched and reached initial, nebulous roots in her heart.

It was with new eyes that she viewed Ian when she came out of the bathroom. She found him in the kitchen beginning the preparations he was familiar with. His shirt-sleeves were rolled up, he wore an apron tied around his waist to protect his navy blue slacks, and he had taken his shoes off. Even in stocking feet and apron he was a tower of dignity, virility and overwhelming masculine beauty. "Thank you," she said simply.

Ian looked at her quizzically. "You are a strange lady, did you know that? In the short space of two hours you have gone from raving mad to blind panic to frenzied pacing to ravenous hunger, and now you come out of the bathroom looking as serene as a new day. What did you do in there, anyway?"

"Just changed my clothes," she said innocently.

"You didn't take a handful of tranquilizers or something rash, did you?"

"Of course not."

"You want to let me in on the secret? If we can bottle it, we'll make a billion dollars."

"You," she said simply, letting it sound half teasing.

"Me?"

Allyn set to work as she spoke. "This is the first time in my adult life that I have come home with a problem and found solace in another person."

Ian grinned broadly. "If you will recall, I have been trying to get through to you just how good we are together."

"Message received," she murmured softly, refrigerating the mousses.

"Let me get this perfectly straight, because I don't want to hang myself in high hopes. You—the reticent Ms. Allyn Danner, woman alone against the world—are admitting that another person—namely me—can be of service, can help you when you're feeling down, can provide something, anything, that you couldn't do all by your lonesome?"

"I think so." She measured the ingredients for the muffins.

"You *think* so. Not complete surrender, but a start." Ian covered the doughs and put them in the second refrigerator.

"I'm not used to sharing my troubles," she admitted to the pans she set out on the counter. "When you give your all to another person and he throws it in your face, you stop short and wonder why. Part of what you come up with—right or wrong—is that maybe you were too needy, that you expected too much of him in return. Self-reliance becomes the antidote for that."

Ian swung her around and into his arms, leaning back against the cupboards and pulling Allyn with him so that her body followed the arch of his. "You are not needy, and you expect less than anyone I have ever known. But needing someone a little does more for the other person than it ever does for you."

"Reed's Lesson In Life, number three?"

"Something like that."

"Well, anyway, thanks for tonight."

"You know, it wouldn't be expecting too much of me to spend the rest of the night soothing you."

"Now that's big of you."

"Yes, I'd say I'm pretty big right now."

"I think sleep is what I need tonight. My head is clogged, and I need it cleared to get things in gear tomorrow."

He trailed light kisses across her forehead and down the length of her nose to the tip. "I think I can manage to keep your mind off business."

"But I won't get much rest out of it."

"True. No arguing that point."

"So get out of here," she said firmly but without malice.

He kissed her lips, slow, sweet, sensuously. "If you're sure..."

"Positive."

Then, more seriously, he asked, "Are you really all right now?"

"As all right as I'm going to be under the circumstances." But brooking no more malingering, she untied the apron from around his waist and wriggled out of his arms. "Thanks for the ice cream."

He slipped his shoes back on, pecked a brief kiss on her lips and winked. "Anytime. Good night, love."

"Good night, Ian," she said softly, fully aware of what she was doing by using his first name at last—allowing a closeness she had held away from him before.

His teasing expression softened, his eyes grew warm, and when he smiled now it was slow and satisfied. "Nice" was his only comment, unwittingly echoing her own earlier thoughts. He kissed her one last time and left.

Allyn closed the door after him and leaned against it. Her business problems weighed on her mind, but they didn't engulf her. For the first time she had the sense that she could handle whatever came her way because of them, and that, at least, felt good. Her feelings for

Ian seemed as if they were under control, so she didn't have the need to deny them, rationalize them or run from them. For the moment she just enjoyed them. Suddenly, even in the face of trouble, all felt right with the world—or if not right, at least not overwhelmingly wrong.

And it was nice. That word again. Nice to feel as if she could take care of herself in the face of both good and bad. Nice to have Ian in her life.

Nice.

Chapter Eleven

Even without the McCauley account, Allyn was up by three the next morning to bake for the remainder of her business. When a knock sounded at her door at three-thirty, she opened it with a pleased smile.

Still resisting the early hour to which Allyn had become accustomed, Ian slumped, mouth agape in a wide yawn, against the plain wooden banister that surrounded the landing outside. At his feet was a large box wrapped in satiny white paper and tied with an enormous red bow.

"You come bearing gifts in the middle of the night?" Allyn teased, as he laboriously leaned over to retrieve it and bring it into the apartment.

"It should be against the law to get up at this hour," he grumbled. Ignoring her question, he set the box on the coffee table and plowed through to the kitchen. From his pocket he took a plastic bag of his specially blended coffee to brew himself a pot, squinting down over a second big yawn that ended with a loud groan.

Allyn closed the door and followed him to the kitchen, but her gaze stayed with the package on the coffee table. "No one said you had to get up and come over here," she reminded, silently refusing to show more curiosity by asking about the gift again.

Facing her across the counter he closed his eyes and let his head fall forward as limply as if he had fallen asleep on his feet. One side of his face flinched upward in a parody of a smile. "It's my only chance to see you. I have to go with Emma and the girls today to get them into a school."

That disappointed Allyn more than she wanted to admit. How easy it was to get used to having him with her all the time. "The girls? School?" she said instead, rounding the counter to spoon dough onto cookie sheets. "I thought they were already in school in Boston?"

"Oh, that's right, I didn't tell you last night. Em brought them back with her. They were having a rough time adjusting, couldn't sleep, nightmares . . . anyway, Emma decided it was better to have them with her right now."

"Poor things," Allyn murmured. "What school?"

"The Wildshores—or Worcestershire or something—Academy. Don't ask me hard questions at this ungodly time of day."

"The Wilshire Academy?"

"Sounds right. Thank God my coffee is ready."

As Ian nearly fell on his morning caffeine fix, Allyn's gaze again wandered to the package. Curiosity got the better of her. "So what's in the box, anyway?"

"Pandora's very question. Beware."

"Okay, wise guy, see if I care." She pointed her nose high in the air and walked around him to put two cookie sheets in the ovens, pretending she didn't see his satisfied smile.

"Tell me quick, what are you doing on the night of October sixth?"

"Flying to Paris for croissants."

"Damn. I should have known. Wouldn't consider canceling, would you?"

"I can't imagine why." She poured steaming mint tea into her cup and leaned nonchalantly against the counter's edge.

"The Harvest Home Ball."

That took the fun out of their game. Allyn stopped playing altogether. "You're kidding?"

"Jon and I were both invited. He's taking Emma. I want you to come with me."

"The Harvest Home Ball," she repeated dimly. "The wingding with movie stars and big wigs flying in from all over the world to donate to cancer research. And you want *me* to go?" Her ending tone of voice illustrated just how ludicrous she found that idea.

Ian paid it no attention as he took her hand and led her to the package. "Before I hear the inevitable barrage of excuses about having nothing to wear and a budget too tight to bear the expense of buying something, open the box."

"It isn't just clothes or budget," Allyn informed him, but as she spoke she pulled the ribbon loose and tore the satiny paper all the same. "I couldn't go to something like that. I wouldn't fit in. The divine gods of status would probably make the whole building shake when I stepped across the threshold. Lights would blow out, music would stop, every voice would go mute and all eyes would turn on me until I took my audacious presence out of there. Oh . . .''

The gown she pulled out of the box was exquisite. A form-fitting creation of hunter-green sequins, it had a high, tight collar, long, snug sleeves, and a slit from the floor-length hem to midthigh. Allyn had only seen such a thing on television. For a moment she was breathless. Awestruck. Overcome. Then she put it back in the box.

"I hope you can get your money back."

Ian took a drink of his coffee, nonplussed by her rejection. "This is purely business, love. Something I have to attend both for Emma's sake and because it's a courtesy to the banks we're handling in the merger—one of them is a major sponsor. You aren't Cinderella going to the ball. You're just helping me out."

"I'm not going."

"Think of it the same as my greasing your pans and unloading your delivery van," he teased with intent.

"Dirty pool, Reed. I never asked for your help."

"But I am asking for yours. This is just not the kind of thing you go to alone."

"You won't be alone. You'll have Emma and Jon."

"It's a couples affair. And since you've brought her up, think of Emma. You know that for Mike's benefit she joined several committees for this cause and now she has somewhat of a stake in the biggest fund-raiser of the year."

"You came in here fully prepared to pull out all the stops, didn't you? The answer is still no."

"Allyn—"

"Don't 'Allyn' me like you're going to put the patience of a saint into practice until I agree. I don't belong in a place like that."

"This isn't the nineteenth century, for crying out loud. No one does or doesn't belong."

"You're saying that to the wrong person, my friend."

"I know your theory on the modern caste system. And I know you see this...maybe even me...as one extreme and you as the other."

"I see it that way because that's the way it is."

"That is not the way it is. Not that I don't understand where this comes from. The kind of divorce you suffered is the ultimate put-down, and I know what that did to your confidence."

"What it did was clarify contemporary lines of social status," she said snidely.

"Your ex-husband really did a convincing number on you, didn't he? Come and let me prove to you that it isn't valid."

Allyn trailed her hand down the dress where the tissue gaped. For a moment she watched the light reflected in the sequins. Playing Cinderella for a night. Dressed up in a gown that probably cost three months' rent. Hobnobbing with celebrities. On the arm of Ian Reed, man extraordinaire. It was tempting.

She pulled her hand away from the dress and firmly closed the box. "It's just not me," she decreed with finality.

"I absolutely have to go to this thing. We'll spend the entire evening with Emma and Jon—both of whom you feel comfortable with. It won't be any different than spending time with them anywhere else."

"Ha!" Allyn blurted. "Half the cast of *Dynasty* showed up last year. I saw it on the news. This is Colorado's version of a big movie premiere. People line the streets hoping for a glimpse of a famous face. Jobs just parking the limos are at a premium because it's a way of getting close to celebrities. Everybody drips furs and diamonds and has vast experience with the press and pictures. How would I know what to do in the middle of something like that?''

"Who do you think wants pictures of arriving investment bankers? We won't be involved in that part of it."

"You can be sarcastic, but I'm not going."

Ian pondered it for a moment before he played his ace in the hole. "Too bad. I was thinking that not only would it be good business for me, but it might be to your advantage, too. Who knows what kind of contacts you could make in a place like that. Money and business get discussed. You meet people, make an impression. They remember you...."

Allyn hesitated. Connections were everything. She might overhear someone talking about wanting to make an investment. She might meet people who could become new accounts. Still, she was skeptical. "What shall I do, carry a bag of cookies around on my arm and pass them out like Little Red Riding Hood?"

Ian smiled slightly, seeing that she was wavering. "I wouldn't do that. No. But you might bring a few business cards in your purse—it's a little flat thing under the dress that matches the shoes. The world is full of possibilities."

"I'd probably be too nervous to remember my name, let alone make any worthwhile impressions or contacts."

"In which case you will just drink champagne until it calms you down, and we'll have a terrific evening."

Withholding final agreement, Allyn lifted a corner of the lid on the box and peeked in at the gown again. It was beautiful. And tempting. And also disconcerting.

How many times had Keith criticized her clothes in that last year before the divorce? Too many. But the time she remembered the most had been for a company Christmas party when he had torn through her closet, discarding everything she owned as too frumpy, too ugly or too cheap looking, and then brought home a dress the next day that was so unlike anything she would ever be caught dead in that she couldn't possibly have worn it. After a huge fight he had gone to the party alone—saying it was probably better that way after all, she was so "out of it," her presence would only make everyone else uncomfortable anyway.

Ian had given this sequined gown in genuine concern for her, not in criticism. And yet it raised such strong memories of Keith. In spite of the spirit in which Ian had given it, somehow this dress made Allyn feel much the same as she once had—inadequate, unable to compete on the same level.

Ian watched the play of emotions that crossed her face. He reached a hand to her chin and turned her face up to his. "I hope I never meet the guy that did this to you. I want you at my side, Allyn. Know that."

Every instinct told her to say no. But when he looked at her that way—so softly, understandingly—she was putty. And, after all, it could be a boon to her business....

She tried for teasing, but her doubts still echoed in her voice. "If I embarrass you and no one in the entire world ever calls you to do another merger, don't blame me."

His lips stretched into a slow, satisfied smile. "Never."

The food court at the Tabor Center was quiet by the time Sylvia bustled in half an hour late for lunch with

Allyn. It was a rare occasion that the two could meet like this, facilitated by the decrease in Allyn's business and the fact that Sylvia had had her own falling-out with Carusoe over his new decline in quality and quit her job. The plump woman's face was pink, her eyes alight as she hurried to where Allyn sat buttering a roll from Au Bon Pain beneath a red and white umbrella.

"I waited for you," Allyn said with a note of chastisement. "When it didn't look like you were going to show up, I went ahead without you."

The pale-haired woman leaned over, peering down her nose at Allyn's soup and sniffing the steam wafting from it. "Tomato Florentine? Great, I'll get a cup and be right back. Eat fast; I have plans for you."

Allyn's roll stopped midway to her gaping mouth with her friend's last words. "What?"

"Eat fast" was all Sylvia would say, though she looked like the cat who'd swallowed the canary. Back in a few minutes with a bowl of soup and two flaky croissants, Sylvia was chewing a bite of one of the pastries by the time she sat down.

"What's up?" Allyn blew on a spoonful of hot soup.

"Good news and better news. Mine first—that's the good news. I got another job."

Allyn's eyebrows arched in surprise. "That's great. I hope it's better than working for Carusoe."

Sylvia waved that away. "I am one of the new chefs for La Maison. Ring any bells?"

"Sure," Allyn said, recognizing the name of a well-known restaurant and catering service. "I tried to get them as an account but they said they have their own dessert chef and wouldn't be interested in ordering from an *outsider*. It's a pretty snooty place. For your sake I hope it gets better if you become an *insider*. How's the money?''

"The money doesn't matter—it's about a ten-percent raise over McCauley's."

"Congratulations," Allyn said, wondering what was inspiring her friend's enthusiasm.

Seeing that Allyn was missing the point, Sylvia sighed elaborately and explained. "La Maison is doing the Harvest Home Ball."

"Ah... Now I understand. That's pretty exciting for you. Funny that that should come up twice in one day."

"Twice? Oh, never mind. You're wrecking my fun. Want to know what the great news is?"

"Sure."

"I went in for the interview this morning and the place was in a mess—that's why I'm late. Seems as though their precious dessert chef works out of his own kitchens, and those kitchens were just closed by the board of health. There were rumors circulating of cigarette butts found in his flour, and all sorts of disgusting things."

Allyn perked up considerably. "And?" she prompted.

"And how would you like to work like a mad fool for the next three days?"

"Give it to me straight, Syl, so I don't imagine it's better than it is."

"They're committed to catering the Harvest Home Ball this Saturday night, and if you want the job of baking desserts for it, you've got it."

Allyn's eyes widened. "You're kidding!"

"The God's honest truth. I talked you up; they remembered you and your stuff and said to bring you over this afternoon."

Allyn deflated back into her chair. "Hot damn," she breathed, stunned. For every door that closed another one opened. And this one was giant-size. La Maison was a prestigious account, and the exposure of catering the desserts for something like the Harvest Home Ball was tremendous.

"What do you say?" Sylvia broke into her reverie.

"I can't believe it. I owe you a big one for this."

"Can you manage it all on such short notice? Maybe it's too much for you."

"I'll do anything I have to."

"I thought you'd say that. Just let me have one more croissant, and I'll take you over."

While Sylvia bought her third pastry Allyn reveled in the news. New connections. Important exposure. She would get her backers and open her own kitchens yet. The Harvest Home Ball.

Ian.

For a moment the butterflies in her stomach turned from excited flutters to tense ones. But only for a moment. Ian would understand. She felt sure of it. In fact he would be thrilled for her.

The Wilshire Academy occupied what had once been a large estate owned by a single family. The main house, an enormous Tudor-style mansion, was used for administration offices, a cafeteria and larger classrooms. The outbuildings—an old carriage house, a garage, servants' quarters, guest cottages, and several other homes that had been built for the family's adult children when they were married—were used as the remaining facilities.

The headmaster was a man named Stuart Markort. He had gone to Harvard with Ian, and while Emma and the girls were being given a tour of the school, Ian and Stuart renewed their acquaintance.

"Imagine running into you in Colorado," Stuart said for the third time as he returned to his paneled office with two cups of coffee. "I had met Emma before while working with her late husband, but I had no idea she was your sister."

"My one and only. I'd appreciate it if you would keep a special eye on my nieces. They've had a rough year."

"Of course. A tragedy, losing Mike Graham. Good man."

"Yes, he was."

"And a fine investment counselor. I especially miss his advice now. My wife inherited quite a large sum of money recently, and I'm at a loss as to what to do with it."

Ian saw it coming. He smiled dispassionately. "Travel. Enjoy it," he suggested.

"Oh, we will. Every intention of it. But there's still a future to look forward to—kids' educations. I wonder if you might have some advice on a good investment?"

"I think what you need, Stu, is a good financial advisor."

"Well, that's probably true. I just thought you might have some inside tips, something we might get in on the ground floor of."

Ian forced patience. It wasn't the first time someone mistook what he did as financial advising. "I deal in mergers of entire companies. I assume you're talking about stocks and bonds, and that's out of my ball-park."

Just then, Emma and the girls returned from their tour and the subject died a natural death. They said their goodbyes and headed home amid Ann's and Elizabeth's excited chatter about the stables and riding lessons and the baby-grand piano in the auditorium.

"Look at those lambs," Elizabeth said enthusiastically as they passed several woolly balls grazing in a field on the way off the grounds. "What do we do with sheep?"

"Maybe they use them for science projects," Ian offered a bit distractedly.

"Oo, ick!" Ann groaned and screwed her face up into a grimace. "You think they dissect them or something?"

Ian laughed at that. "Raise them, watch them grow, maybe shear them and learn what to do with the wool, but I'm sure they don't dissect them, no."

"Think we get to take them home at the end of the year?" Elizabeth said hopefully.

Emma laughed. "What would Brit do with a sheep?"

That was enough to send both girls into roaring giggles loud enough to make the adults in the front seat flinch.

"Quiet, girls," Emma chastised, then turned to Ian as her daughters put their heads together for more confidential discussion of the boys at the Wilshire Academy.

As he drove, Ian's mind was on Allyn and her business. He was genuinely sorry her arrangement with Carusoe hadn't panned out.

And yet, maybe it was for the best.

Marriage seemed like a constant thought the past few days, more so since learning about her deep desire for a family. He loved Allyn. He believed she loved him—even though she was reticent to admit it. Had she acquired investors and expanded, it might have put her personal life on hold indefinitely in the crush of added work. As it was, at least there wouldn't be an increase in her work, leaving them the opportunity to go on as they were, growing closer to coming to terms with a future together.

Maybe this was fate's hand after all.

Ian felt hopeful.

Allyn was on the telephone when Ian arrived at the garage apartment at five that afternoon. On the island counter at which she sat was a tablet and several loose papers already torn off, scrawled with notes and lists. As she finished her conversation Ian glanced at the unusual disarray, wondering what had inspired the mess and the high color that illuminated her skin to a glow and made those marvelous blue eyes of hers sparkle.

Replacing the receiver, she spun around on her barstool and hopped down. "Iced tea?"

"Thanks. What's going on around here?"

Allyn's face was alight with a smile as she took down two Styrofoam cups and filled them. "You will never believe it."

Ian watched her and laughed. "I don't know what it is, but I hope it lasts. Do you know how beautiful you are when you're happy like this?"

She laughed back. "Nope. And I don't have time to look, either. I feel like a dessert mogul."

"Carusoe dropped dead from an arrogance attack, and you were left beneficiary of his life insurance. You won the state lottery. You just discovered the existence of a scholarship for beginning bakers. What?"

"Better than all of the above. Well, maybe not better than winning the lottery. Opportunity has knocked on my door. La Maison—a very prestigious restaurant and catering service—has just hired me to do the desserts for none other than the Harvest Home Ball.'' She handed him the cup victoriously.

"Ah," Ian mused, nodding in understanding but sounding short on enthusiasm as he accepted the tea. "It's a big account, I take it."

Belatedly she recognized his reserve and remembered their date for that same occasion. "You understand, don't you, Ian? Going as a guest is nothing compared to the exposure I'll get standing behind the table while people actually taste my stuff."

He frowned at a new thought. "You're serving, too?"

"Not really serving, no. I'll be in the kitchen getting everything ready, and then, once it's all set out, I'll just observe and make sure I'm on hand with my business cards. If I can pull this off, getting backing to expand will be all the more important, and I really need to be there in a business capacity, to make contacts with investors on my own terms."

"What do you mean, *on your own terms*?"

She shrugged, looking off over her shoulder. "I won't be meeting people under false pretenses, pretending to be something I'm not, depending on my connection with you for introductions...." She looked him squarely in the eye. "It's important to me to do this on my own."

He gave a sardonic laugh. "And having you at my side is important to me. I was counting on you."

"It's just a date," she reminded him, with the beginning edge of anger in her voice.

"No, it isn't just a date." There was more anger in his calm tone than had he shouted.

"What is it, then?"

"It's an occasion. A special occasion. Something I was looking forward to. Counting on. Planning on. Something that's good for *my* business."

"Well, of course you'll still go." She didn't understand his anger.

"And I wanted you to go with me. Not be there working in the kitchen."

His anger added a condemning tone to his voice and his words seemed to confirm Allyn's worst fears about the differences in their backgrounds and life-styles. "I thought you, of all people, would understand," she said, her voice echoing caution. She felt herself drawing away from him as if he had suddenly become someone she didn't know.

"And I thought for once you were going to put something besides business first." He gave a short, mirthless chuckle. "I'll tell you something, lady. Ambition doesn't have to be an obsession."

Allyn had never seen anger in Ian. It took her off guard. She defended herself by striking back. "Maybe what we really have here is the fact that it embarrasses you to have anyone know you're hanging out with the help. Isn't that the real reason for you getting mad about this? You even went to the trouble of picking out what I should wear so my *lesser status* wouldn't be glaringly evident."

His finger shot out at her. "It's you who has that class hang-up. Don't pin it on me. I bought the damn dress to save you the expense, and you know it."

She did, but at that moment it didn't matter. She was hurt that he had taken this tack—angry that he had burst her bubble and made her feel guilty. "My business is important to me. Every bit as important as yours is to you."

"You're wrong there. Yours is by far more important to you than mine is to me. I've learned the pitfalls in the road you're traveling. A road that ends with an empty, shallow existence if you don't stop racing down it long enough to have a life besides."

"Now you sound like Sylvia and my family."

"With good reason—it's the truth. Like it or not, Allyn, we have a relationship. It's special. It's good. Stop and realize that I can give you what you really want."

"In the first place," she said with deadly calm, "if what I want is *given* to me I run the risk of having it taken away as easily. And what exactly is it that you think I want?"

"The same thing I do—marriage, babies, a family. I know you gave your ex all of yourself and he took it for granted, put it down, trashed it. The man was a fool. But don't confuse me with him. A woman who gives all of herself is what I've been looking for. Something I will never take for granted. Take a risk and give to me what you gave to him."

For a moment Allyn merely stared at him, stunned. Then she said, very quietly, very firmly. "No. I will never give up everything for a man again."

Ian threw what remained of his tea into the sink so fiercely that the ice cubes hit like hail. "I didn't say I wanted you to give up everything. I just said I wanted you—all of you. You keep so many barriers around yourself you might as well wear armor, and this damn business is the worst of it. It's your escape from life, from love. I'm offering you what you really want, and you're letting the past and fear refuse us both."

Allyn's hands went to her hips, her knuckles white. "My business isn't an escape. You've grabbed onto the revelation of my wanting kids and let it drown out everything else. It isn't that simple or that one-sided. There are two parts, Ian—two sides. Okay, I may have been wrong to ignore the side of myself that wants a baby. But you want me to deny the other side now, to cast it off just because you've come on the scene. I have to be self-sufficient and self-supporting. That is every bit as important to me as kids. Maybe it's not as emotionally obvious, but it's just as important."

"Is it, Allyn? Or is it just that you're too damned afraid to live a real life? You're carrying around so much excess baggage from your past that you can't have a present, much less a future."

"This is not about the past or fear. You just don't see it."

"No, I don't. It's only fear I see—fear of love, of trusting me, of opening yourself up and letting me in. Fear that if you do, you'll lose everything again."

"It isn't fear," she insisted too loudly. "It's a lesson I learned the hard way. It taught me that I need a safety net to protect myself. That safety net is my business."

"You don't need a safety net with me. Your business can take a more realistic perspective, a back seat to the rest of your life the way it should, rather than being the obsession it is."

"In other words, it should be my little hobby," she said snidely. "Good God, you're as arrogant as Keith if you reduce everything I've done to something to fill the time until you happen by to offer me your life. Strike another blow for my unbelievable naïveté. I actually thought you respected what I do. I really believed you were as interested in my success as I was. But you were just humoring me. I'll bet you thought I was done in when the deal with Carusoe fell through, didn't you? My little hobby would die a natural death and I could devote myself to you, instead.

"Do you think I don't see how much you'd like to have control over me, over my life? To manipulate me into getting what you want? Colorado Springs, the dress, even your very presence in my day-to-day life, in my business, was all because *you* decided that was the way it was going to be. Had I failed because of Carusoe it would have been clear sailing for you, wouldn't it? But instead, you came in here today and found out that wasn't going to happen, and it made you mad."

Ian's anger sparked hot again. "Or maybe I hoped that just once your feelings for me would be strong enough to take precedence over your business. I'll tell you what I think, Danner—" he held his empty cup up for illustration "—I think you want a Styrofoam man— disposable. Use him for what you need for the moment and throw him out the way you do your cups and plates. No responsibilities, no commitments, no obligations, no ties. Just use and toss."

"Better that than being the one who's used and discarded."

For a moment her words echoed like a slap. Then, very quietly, very soberly, Ian said, "Well, that makes everything pretty clear, doesn't it? I'll take it as advice."

He handed her the cup and left.

Chapter Twelve

October third brought a gust of cold autumn weather as a blessing. For the next three days the ovens ran day and night, heating the small garage apartment like a blast furnace.

Adrenaline kept Allyn going through those three days of nonstop work. She didn't sleep more than two hours a night, and if the delectable concoctions she produced for the Harvest Home Ball would put five pounds on everyone who indulged, they took seven off of Allyn. For the remainder of that week she skipped her office rounds and did the absolute bare minimum for her other restaurant accounts in order to bake for the Saturday-night fête. Days were spent by herself, bustling around like a chicken with her head cut off while her brother Tim ran between his job at the health club and making her deliveries. Evenings found the small apartment brimming with people as Allyn's family rallied round to help. Even Emma and the twins pitched in.

The only person conspicuously absent was Ian.

She should have been too busy to care. She should have been glad that he left her alone. She should have been relieved that he had finally accepted the fact that her business was the most important thing in her life.

But she wasn't.

Her temper was short, her patience thin. She knew that if everyone who lent a hand didn't love her they would have abandoned her. As it was, they excused her abrasiveness, accepting her oft-repeated apologies with murmurings of how they understood the pressure she was under and how important this was to her. She also knew that when they didn't think she could hear, they discussed the fact that the rift with Ian was a strong contribution to her mood. And everyone had his own opinion as to whether that was a good sign—illustrating how much she cared for him—or a bad sign, indicating it was irreconcilable. Regardless of what her friends and family whispered about, Allyn made it known that to her the subject of her and Ian was taboo.

Only to herself did she admit that she was all too familiar with the feeling of heaviness that sat on her chest, the lack of hunger and the inability to force down more than meager amounts of food. She knew well the frenzied need to keep busy, the exhaustion that put her to sleep within three seconds of getting into bed at night followed by that jolt of unexplainable panic that woke her and kicked her out of bed after so little sleep. None of it came from pressure or tension about business. It was her response to pain. To loss. To grief.

Emma was the last to leave after midnight on Friday. Everything was under control, ready for the last-minute touches that would be done Saturday before transporting it all to Merchant's Hall.

Allyn walked her landlady to the door, yawning behind her hand as she went. "I'm beat," she informed her needlessly.

Emma reached up to untie the ribbon that held her own brown hair, shaking it free. "Desserts for eight hundred people in three days' time? No wonder."

"I couldn't have managed it without you guys helping. I really appreciate it."

"I think we all had a good time. Of course, if your sister-in-law doesn't watch out, Ann is going to steal Tim away from her. I think my daughter is in the throes of a major crush. She followed him around like a shadow."

Allyn smiled at the thought. "He loved it. She was a boost to his ego."

"I'm serious about replacing that bowl Elizabeth broke. Something that size must cost a fortune, and I don't want you paying for it."

"Cheap, compared to what it would have cost me to pay for all the help."

"But one I can afford better than you can. Besides, from what I understand, between what Ian's broken playing baker's assistant and this, you're going to have to take out a loan to restock your kitchen."

At the mention of Ian's name and the spurred memory of him working for her, Allyn's features tightened. She escaped her friend's scrutiny by bending over for an impromptu toe-touch meant to look as if she were stretching a kink out of her back. But when she straightened up again, she could tell by the look on

Emma's face and the intent way she continued to watch her, that the other woman had brought up Ian's name for a reason.

"He'll be glad to hear you made it. He's been pulling for you."

"Yep, we made it all right." Allyn put her hands on either side of her waist and did torso twists.

Emma was not going to be deterred. "He's also been worrying about you. The girls and I get grilled every time we come home from here. He'll be waiting up for me tonight and won't let me go to bed until I give him a full report—how you are, if you ate, if you look tired. He's worse than a mother."

"Oh no, I forgot to even offer anyone a sandwich again, didn't I?" Allyn slid her hands around to her rump and pulsed backward.

"He's hurting, you know."

That stopped the calisthenics. Allyn swallowed hard and looked off to a high corner of the apartment. Was she playing Keith's role? That was a thought too ugly to bear. She swallowed again before she could find her voice. "I didn't mean to hurt him."

"I never thought you did."

"I'm sorry," she whispered. Where had tears come from? She fought them by holding her breath as Emma stepped out the door.

"I just thought you should know," she said as she headed down the stairs. "He's hurting. You're hurting. Seems sort of silly to me."

Allyn closed the door and locked it. Necessity forced the air out of her lungs in a convulsive sob that released the tears in her eyes, too. Her chest heaved again and again.

She took it as confirmation that love meant pain—something to avoid at all costs.

Jon's silver stretch limousine was appropriate for the formality of the Harvest Home Ball. The interior was plush gray velvet, and Ian purposely took the seat opposite his sister so that Jon could sit beside Emma. As the two chatted amiably, Ian stared out the smoke-tinted window at the light, dry powder of the season's first snow. Eighty degrees on Tuesday, snowing on Saturday. That was Colorado. In spite of this early storm—though it was so light the term didn't really apply—a mild winter was being predicted. Ian wondered if he would be around to see for himself.

He could leave on Monday if he wanted. There was a deal brewing in Bogotá that would keep him occupied for the next several months. At least if he were busy the days wouldn't go as slowly as these past three had—long, tedious, miserable.

Time and space, that's what he had decided to give Allyn. But he was afraid it wouldn't matter. Her past had left palpable scars.

"I met Stuart Markort's wife, Evelyn, at school yesterday," Emma said, breaking into his maudlin thoughts. "She mentioned that Stuart had asked you about investment advice."

Before Ian could answer Jon joined in. "We went to Harvard with a Markort, didn't we? Tall drink of water, deadly serious."

"The same," Ian said, still distracted by his own dark mood.

"You know," Emma said. "I've been thinking about it since I spoke to Evelyn, and I wonder if they might be interested in backing Allyn."

Ian's attention was fully on his sister now. Her suggestion had the same effect on him as fingernails scraping blackboard. "You're talking about venture capital, Emma. The Markorts mean stocks, bonds—that sort of thing. In fact, when I said that wasn't what I handled, the conversation ended."

"It is a thought, though," Jon agreed. "Maybe you ought to suggest it, Ian."

Irritation at his friend sparked in Ian. Jon would agree with anything Emma said. He frowned at his friend, his tone cool. "You know as well as I do that suggestion implies responsibility and if they lose a dime they'll hang it on me."

Jon cocked his head at his friend. "You don't think she's a good risk then?"

The two men stared at each other, Ian unaccountably angry and Jon amused by it. It was Emma who picked up the conversation. "Of course Allyn is a good risk. She'd work herself to death rather than see that business go under. And after tonight she'll no doubt get this La Maison account and a lot more. She'll really need the money to expand just to keep up with it all. There's no risk that I can see."

Jon raised a challenging eyebrow at Ian. "That's about how I see it, too. As well as the fact that she has a great product."

"I didn't have so much as an inkling that he was interested in something like this."

"But it's an idea," Jon persisted. "You know as well as I do that sometimes people see putting their money one place and a simple suggestion can change their perspective and lead them in a whole different direction. If your involvement with Allyn bothers you, I'd be happy to throw it out to Markort and take responsibility."

Ian's anger ignited into full-blown rage. White-hot. And with it went alarms. Something was wrong here. "I need to think about it," he ground out. He opened the glass that separated them from the driver and ordered the car to stop. "Merchant's Hall is only about six blocks away—I'm going to walk it and meet you there."

"It's snowing," Emma said in her mother voice.

Jon patted her hand. "He'll be fine. A little cold, fresh air helps clear complicated financial—and personal—webs."

Ian stepped out of the car into the season's first snow. Downtown Denver's streetlights illuminated the glitter of snowflakes. The air was crisp. Clusters of people stood in the doorways of tall marble banks and black glass office buildings waiting for buses. A few flipped up coat collars, plunged their hands into the warmth of pockets and walked briskly along the wide sidewalks.

A black cashmere evening coat, a white silk scarf wrapped around his throat, and gloves kept Ian oblivious to the cold, and he noticed neither people nor places as he walked. Instead his mind was filled with thoughts about Allyn, himself and his inappropriate response to the idea of steering the Markorts' money into Danner's Decadent Desserts.

Why, he wondered, had it been a subject to spark such fury in him unless he actually was guilty of Allyn's accusation that he wanted her to fail?

Did he?

Not consciously.

She had worked hard to make a success of her business. He admired that. Her drive, her ambition, her energy, were all part of what had attracted him to her in the first place, part of why he loved her. He had great respect for what she had done in taking hold of her life after the hideousness that had touched her, and building something from there. Failure was the last thing he would wish on her.

Yet expansion meant even more demands on her, on her time. It meant her business taking a bigger place in her life than it already had, making her more involved, more preoccupied than she already was.

Expansion might mean she would choose Danner's Decadent Desserts over a life with him.

And he didn't want that, either.

As he entered Merchant's Hall, Ian admitted to himself that Jon and Emma had been right. In his experienced hands, the Markorts could be convinced to invest in Allyn. And he would run the risk of never having what he wanted most—Allyn herself.

Or he could leave things as they were.

It was all in his hands.

In order to camouflage the fact that as an exhibition hall, Merchant's natural ambience was that of a warehouse, the lighting was kept to the dim glow of candles on each linen tableclothed table and golden lanterns strung around the room's perimeter. Potted trees around the outer walls, their leaves a brilliant autumn yellow and vibrant rust, provided further decoration. Painted scenery lined the cement walls, succeeding in giving the place a more polished atmosphere.

In the small space assigned as the kitchen, La Maison's staff of chefs, assistant chefs, busboys and waitresses crowded around long worktables and bustled in and out of swinging doors to stock the buffet tables. In the bright light of this section of the Merchant's center, Allyn meticulously sliced the brownies, tortes and mousses herself, arranging them on each plate with a

simple garnish of three fresh raspberries set on a sprig
of mint leaves. Cookies and muffins had already been
placed on white paper doilies on silver trays, and busboys hurriedly grabbed them up and carted them out.
When Allyn's work space became backlogged, she
hoisted two trays herself and took them out. At the long
buffet tables waitresses served in formal black-and-
white maids' uniforms. It was one of these girls who
took the replacements for a dessert array that was fast
dwindling.

"I can't keep up with them," the waitress complained, but it was music to Allyn's ears.

For a moment she paused to watch a line of people
choose from the newly arrived tray, reveling in the
compliments she overheard. And then she glanced out
into the sea of faces and without purposely looking for
him, found Ian.

Dressed in a black tuxedo, his pleated silk shirt
starkly white, he looked magnificent. Somewhere in the
time they had grown close, Allyn had lost sight of his
innate dignity, had come to take it for granted. It struck
her again now. Power. Strength. Confidence. Dignity.
The man radiated them. Only now she knew too well the
soft, gentle, warm side of him, too. It made her feel
worse. She suddenly realized that the frightening thing
about her feelings during the past three days' sepa-
ration was that as much as she missed him physically—
his touch, his kisses, his arms, as much as her body
craved the feel of his, the comfort of him—more, she
missed the man himself. She missed his humor, his
company, his understanding, his genuine kindness. And
that was not something she had felt even in the ending
of a relationship of longevity with Keith O'Neal.

Maybe she was wrong in burying her feelings for Ian, in rejecting them and him with them. Maybe there was more to this relationship than there had been with Keith. Maybe she should take the risk....

But as she stood behind the buffet table looking out at the guests, it was hard to believe there was hope for them.

At five hundred dollars a plate, the crowd was culturally elite—the cream of what Keith O'Neal aspired to, what he emulated in his leased car and cashmere socks. Within this group Ian was the epitome of sophistication. He was a cosmopolitan man. He was the model of what Keith O'Neal wanted to be.

And there was Allyn, in her best corduroy slacks and white blouse, behind the buffet table. If the difference between her and Keith had been pronounced, then the difference between her and Ian was a chasm, she thought. If she couldn't even pass muster with the imitation, how could she ever be a match for the original?

Perversely torturing herself, she stayed frozen in place, watching him, mentally trying to staunch the feelings she had for him and say goodbye.

With Jon, Emma introduced Ian to one group of people and then another. Even from a distance, Allyn could see Ian's charm as he smiled and greeted his sister's friends. Allyn's heart was in her throat. She had thought Keith's betrayal, the divorce, the miscarriage, were as complicated as life would ever be. But here she was in love with a man who wanted things she couldn't give, a man miles and miles above the one she had already not been good enough for. And everything was complicated all over again.

It can't be, she told herself. Turn and walk away.

But before she followed her own orders Allyn realized he was headed toward her.

Stay away, Ian. Just leave it the way it is, she thought in a panic. And then she spun around and nearly ran back into the kitchen.

But Ian evidently didn't see the same clear borderlines dividing them. He followed right behind.

"Allyn." He came all the way to her table, ignoring the fact that she was ignoring him.

"You can't come in here," she said in a sharp whisper, glancing furtively around at the interested audience looking up from their work in the brightly lit space.

"Why can't I?" he asked logically, seeing the same thing she did and not giving it a second thought.

"This is the kitchen. It's for the catering staff, not the guests," she said through gritted teeth.

He frowned at her and whispered sarcastically, "If I put on an apron, will you talk to me?"

"No. Get out of here."

"I have some things to say to you."

"We said all we needed to the other night. I'm working, and you don't belong back here." To illustrate her point, she began slicing a pan of macaroon brownies with a long knife.

"Don't start this ridiculous status thing again."

"You're embarrassing me."

"Then let's find a quiet corner where we can talk."

"I'm working," she repeated firmly.

"Your work is done. Anyone can cut those damn things."

Allyn bristled. "It's important to me that everything is just right."

"I guarantee that what I have to say to you is more important."

"To you, maybe."

"Dammit, Allyn, this has to do with business. I have a bloody investor for the almighty Danner's Decadent Desserts. How's that?"

Good and bad. It stunned her and disappointed her at the same time. Had he only come to talk to her about business? "Oh" was all that she could manage. She wiped her hands, and asked one of the kitchen staff to finish cutting the brownies for her. Then she faltered, wondering suddenly where they could go. Dressed so informally, conferencing with Ian among the guests would draw as much attention as his presence in the kitchen did.

Ian had her hesitation pegged the moment he saw it. He took her elbow and steered her back through the doors into the party. "The people I want you to meet are guests."

Allyn held back. "If someone approaches me, it's one thing, but I can't go out there and solicit the guests to gain a backer. I could lose this job over something like that."

"Fine," Ian said curtly. "Then I'll bring them to you."

He was gone before she could say more. Not knowing what to do, Allyn went back into the kitchen. Her mind was in a jumble and it didn't improve when Ian reappeared with two more of the guests in tow. Without waiting for a suggestion, he led the way to the staff rest rooms. He left Allyn, Stuart Markort and his wife, Evelyn, in the hallway that separated the men's from the women's while he blocked the opening and turned away anyone who wandered there to use the facilities.

Allyn didn't know what to say. It was Evelyn Markort who broke the ice.

"We've inherited a substantial amount of money recently, and Ian seems to think that investing in your business is as good as putting it in IBM stock. He said we couldn't go wrong, and now that I've sampled your creations, I have to agree."

Allyn drew a deep breath, tried hard to block out the fact that Ian was so near and briefly outlined her expansion plans. It took a mere fifteen minutes of listening to her sales pitch for the Markorts to decide they were definitely interested and arrange a meeting to discuss the details. As fast as it had begun, it was over, and Allyn was left alone with Ian.

"Thank you," she said quietly, guiltily.

Ian continued to block the end of the hallway so no one could get to the bathrooms and Allyn couldn't escape back into the kitchen. His deep voice filled the small space and wrapped around her. "It was a show of good faith."

A flurry of emotions washed through Allyn. She knew she couldn't look at him and still maintain her resolve to resist what she felt. So instead she nervously turned her head to stare at the wall. "A show of good faith?" she repeated dimly.

"You were right, I was reducing what you do and want to a hobby status because of my own selfishness. I admit that I wouldn't have regretted it if Carusoe had ruined you, if you had turned to me and we had been able to ride off into the sunset together so I could have you all to myself. But that isn't what happened and I'm willing to adjust to it."

"What does that mean?" Allyn asked carefully.

Ian glanced at their location, standing between two rest rooms in a dingy hallway. "Somehow I think this would be more picturesque in other surroundings. I'm in love with you, Allyn. I want you to marry me, to have my babies. I introduced you to the Markorts to prove to you that I can accept your ambition, your drive to succeed on your own as the other side of that coin. I made a mistake before. And even if it was an unconscious mistake, I'm not proud of it. Everyone has selfish thoughts; it's human nature. What counts is whether or not you act on them, whether or not you let them rule. Don't crucify me for my subconscious thoughts and feelings. Consider my actions."

Had it been another time, another place, Allyn might have lost sight of the rest of what made their relationship hopeless. But as if fate were determined to remind her of the past, it wasn't another time or place. It was here, in the middle of the most glaring example of their difference.

Her eyes filled. Her throat was so tight she could hardly breathe. She loved him so much. . . .

Allyn drew up straight, belligerent. She forced her voice to be abrasive. "I appreciate the introduction and the endorsement with the Markorts. But beyond that it's better if we just let well enough alone."

Ian let out a derisive sound—part laugh, part sigh. "Then it isn't only the present, the business, your ambition, is it? We're back to the past. Tell me this isn't about fear now, Allyn. Fear of loving, of trusting, of being hurt again. Because when it's all said and done, that's where we are."

"Where we are," she said cuttingly, her voice knife-edged with pain and regret, "is working from a basis of past experience—my past experience. We're too different. Opposites may attract, but in the end it doesn't work out. And we are definitely at opposite ends." She accentuated this last with a nod at the expensive tuxedo he wore. "I've found my niche, Ian, and it was hard-won. This side of the buffet table is where I want to stay. I don't want to try to mold myself to fit the other side. Not even for you."

"Dammit, Allyn," he shouted and began to reach for her. When she stepped back away from him he stretched his arms out to the sides instead and formed a T in the hall opening, leaning forward. He lowered his voice. "For a smart woman, that is the most idiotic thing I have ever heard."

"I'm a plain person," she said angrily. "I lead a plain life. That's what makes me happy. Just leave me alone with it."

"*Alone* being the operative word here. Protective isolation."

"It's my choice." Sparks of challenge shot from her eyes.

"And there's nothing I can do about it, is that what you're saying?"

She verified it with the arch of an eyebrow and the tilt of her chin, because her throat was too clogged with tears to say anything.

"Well, it's a bad choice I think we're both going to regret."

He pushed himself away forcefully and left, his coattails billowing out behind him, his heels clacking loudly on the cement floor.

For Allyn, regret was not something that would come in time. It was already here. But she had done what she felt she had to do.

Chapter Thirteen

Knowing she would need to work into the morning hours at the Harvest Home Ball, Allyn had done the unthinkable—she had canceled out on all of her Sunday accounts. By five in the morning she regretted it.

She had expected to be so exhausted she would sleep like a baby from the time she got home until maybe seven or eight o'clock. Instead, she hadn't been able to close her eyes, spending the night pacing, thinking about Ian and wishing she had work to distract her.

Then again, work hadn't managed to distract her in the past four days, had it? Disturbing thought.

Once she had gotten on her feet after the miscarriage and started Danner's Decadent Desserts, work had used up so much of her energy that she'd had little left over for suffering or lamenting the end of her marriage. But this time it wasn't accomplishing that same kind of escape. This time, no matter how busy she was, her thoughts were still preoccupied with Ian. And the intense sense of loss she felt had nothing to diffuse it.

Still, she had been right to sever their relationship, she told herself over and over again. There was safety in being alone in life. You learned to depend only on yourself, and then you were never disappointed. Never hurt.

So how come she was alone and hurt at the same time?

"That's what you get for letting someone get even this close," she berated herself aloud, swallowing back the sting of tears. "Another lesson, Al: other people may be tough enough to have flings. But you aren't. From now on, steer clear of *any* entanglements."

At six she decided lackadaisically to scrub the bathroom. Anything was better than pacing.

From the bathroom she moved on to dusting, then straightening cupboards that didn't need it, then mopping the kitchen floor. By the time that was finished she had convinced herself she was better off without him; that she didn't love Ian all that much....

And then there was a knock on her door.

The bucket she was about to empty dropped out of her hand and splashed all over the clean floor. She barely noticed it in the rush of hope that raced through her. Her glance jerked to the clock. Seven o'clock. Who would it be but Ian? Her heartbeat sped up, and suddenly she felt warm, excited, alive, vibrant. Nothing mattered but that she would open the door and there he'd be....

But it wasn't Ian who stood on the landing outside.

It was Sylvia.

Allyn deflated.

As she came in, Sylvia explained the unusual visit. "I didn't think you'd be able to sleep in. I took a chance, bought doughnuts and thought I'd see if your lights were on before heading to work. I'm dying to hear about last night."

For one moment Allyn peered out the door as if she might still see Ian. Then she closed it, disappointment dropping her spirits even lower than they'd been.

"Pour tea, will you? I have a mess to mop up," she said as she moved to do just that.

"So tell me," her friend prompted once she had taken the box of doughnuts and two cups of tea into the living room, seated herself on the floor near the coffee table and dunked her first cinnamon twist. "You can clean and talk at the same time. And then I have a juicy story for you, too."

Allyn began with details of the Harvest Home Ball, the guests, the celebrities she had seen, meeting the Markorts and their interest in investing in her. She knew she was in deep trouble when even the thought of expansion didn't make her feel better, and from there, by the time she had joined her friend on the floor, she ended up confiding what had happened with Ian.

As if she were stalling for time to gauge her words, Sylvia left Allyn sitting there and replenished her tea. When she came back she spoke in a voice she made quiver like an old woman's. "Time for Aunt Sylvia to open her big mouth and say what she thinks."

"I know what you think," Allyn grumbled. "That I'm crazy."

"You got it," she said in her normal voice. "But first I'm going to tell you my gossip. Are you ready?"

Allyn watched her friend, confused. "I think you've lost me."

"Storytime first. Howie and I met good old Keith O'Neal at the movies last night. I think the man will air his dirty laundry to anyone who will listen, and we got an earful. Hang on, this is amazing. Seems as though the marriage of Keith and the bimbette hit a rocky road."

"Not too amazing," Allyn said wryly. "The only thing they knew about each other was that they were both liars and cheats."

"True. Anyway, it seems as though once more some little tail wagger caught old Keith's attention and, yes, you guessed it, *this* time it was true love. He was on the verge of breaking the news to bimbette number one— also known as the second Mrs. O'Neal—when he came home and found her in bed with none other than the husband she had deserted for Keith in the first place."

"Good grief," Allyn breathed. It did elicit a laugh from her, though.

"Wait, this is particularly choice. Keith was outraged, devastated, totally stunned—and all of a sudden he realized that no, he didn't really love the new bimbette, he wanted to save his marriage to the old one. Only problem was that the second Mrs. O'Neal didn't want him. She was in re-love with her first husband. She walked out."

"Aww, poor Keith."

"Wait, I'm not through. When we met him last night he had this big bandage over his nose. It seems as if Keith kept trying to persuade the sweet thing to come back to him. The first husband got fed up, went to

Keith's office, punched him in the face and broke his nose.''

''Not in keeping with the professional image, I wouldn't think.''

''Hardly. While Keith has been trying to win back the bimbette, he's also royally screwed up a major project he was responsible for. So now Mr. Big Deal is out a girlfriend, a second wife, has a broken nose and is in jeopardy of losing his job. Funny thing, too—he can't believe all this is happening to him. As if he doesn't have it coming.'' Sylvia smiled with satisfaction. ''Couldn't have happened to a nicer guy.''

For the moment Allyn's mood was lightened by the pure absurdity of her friend's telling. ''That was a pretty good story,'' she admitted.

''There's a point to it.''

''Which is?'' Allyn even managed a bite of a doughnut and a sip of her now tepid tea.

Sylvia sobered, her tone of voice turned more serious. ''Just after your divorce was final, when Keith kept saying he didn't care what he took as his half as long as he could just get out, you said something to me that blew me away. You said you didn't know how to handle being someone so revolting that Keith would give up everything you had together, go to any extremes just to get rid of you. It stuck with me because I couldn't believe that somewhere in your mind you were taking all the blame, not to mention that it was such an awful thing to say about yourself, and a worse thing to feel. It tore me apart to hear it.'' Sylvia's voice cracked and her eyes filled. Allyn looked away before her own did the same.

Her friend ate another doughnut and continued. "Over the last two years I've thought that feeling of being loathsome was responsible for a lot of what kept you from ever looking for another man—that you were so down on yourself you figured that if by some chance a man did love you again, he'd eventually find you as 'revolting' as Keith did."

Allyn spoke to her bent knees. "You always surprise me, do you know that? You go along seeming to take everything at face value and then come up with too much insight for my own good."

"I'm not finished. What my 'insight' is seeing now is a new twist to this. And it really stinks."

"If it stinks, don't tell me."

"I'm going to tell you, because it's doing more damage and it needs to be stopped. You've found a terrific guy—you know it, I know it, everybody knows it. He loves you and you love him, and things could be great. Only the better it gets, the closer you think he's coming to seeing how revolting you are. So what do you do? Beat him to the punch. You reject him before he has the chance to reject you."

"Thank you, Dr. Freud."

"It's the truth."

"If it's the truth it just proves I'm as revolting as Keith thought."

With a mock shriek, Sylvia reached over, took Allyn by the shoulders, and shook her. "*Keith O'Neal* was the creep—not you. It was *his* loss, *his* stupidity, *his* shallowness, *his problem*. You were just his victim—no more to blame than if you lock your doors before you leave home and while you're gone someone smashes a

window, breaks in and steals everything. Is it *your* fault
that you got robbed?"

"No."

"I rest my case. Except for one thing. If you were to
blame, if you were so revolting, how come he's right
back in the middle of it all again? He cheated on this
one, too. He was ready to dump her, too. He must have
found her revolting, too. Like a flash she wasn't good
enough for him, either—until he thought someone else
wanted her, and then she was great again. This is not a
person whose judgment of anyone or anything can be
valid. He's crackers." Sylvia got up, brushed doughnut
crumbs off her lap and picked up her purse. "I have to
get to work. But mark my words, kid, if you let this guy
go you'll be sorry. And you will have let good old Keith
rob you of more than he already has."

Allyn didn't get up to walk her friend to the door. She
didn't even say goodbye. She just sat where she was on
the floor, staring into space.

Strangely, Keith's problems brought her none of the
satisfaction they would have if they'd happened in the
first year after the divorce, that first year of her own
misery when he was happily enjoying the new life he
thought he deserved. But now, good or bad, she honestly didn't care what happened to him. It did serve as
an illustration of where the problems had really origin-
ated, though—the same immaturity, the same infantile
infatuation, that had caused it to happen once, caused
it to happen again. And it would probably keep on
happening.

Tacky. Tawdry. Immoral. Ugly. Just plain classless.

And *that* was what she had been feeling not good enough for? *That* was what she had been feeling inadequate in comparison to?

Sitting there alone, Allyn laughed.

It was Keith O'Neal who wasn't good enough for her, not the other way around. Ian had said it once before, but she hadn't really believed it then. Now, picturing the whole sordid scene with the second wife, it struck her as the truth. And she deserved someone better than that.

She deserved Ian.

He had been right about it being fear that held her back. But not fear of commitment or trust as much as fear of being found out. Maybe that was why the class difference she thought was so glaringly evident escaped his notice. It wasn't her social class she'd feared he would chafe at, it was his seemingly inevitable discovery that she was the same revolting, inadequate person Keith had discovered in her. But that revolting, inadequate person didn't exist—any more than Keith's deep love for either of the bimbettes had been real. They were all figments of his imagination. In that moment Allyn realized that she had been carrying around an image of herself that was nothing more than Keith's justification for his affairs, for his fantasies, for trashing something of value solely for the sake of adolescent infatuation.

With the realization a deadweight was lifted from her shoulders. It was safe to let Ian in, to love him, because what he saw in her was the genuine article, good and bad, and he loved her anyway.

And she loved him.

She could have the security of her business—he had already conceded that point. She could have her independence. And she could have them both with Ian. Love didn't have to mean pain.

Revitalized, Allyn sprung up from the floor. She would shower, change into her best clothes, and find that man before it was too late.

It was already too late when Allyn crossed the yard half an hour later. Through the kitchen window she saw Emma making coffee. She tapped on the glass.

"Allyn," Emma said tentatively. "I'm surprised to see you."

"Is Ian up yet?" she answered anxiously.

Emma frowned. "Up and gone, I'm afraid." She made it sound ominous.

"Gone?"

"Allyn..." Emma sighed, obviously reluctant to tell her what was going on.

Allyn's spirits dropped like a rock. Too much damage. She had rejected him once too often. It served her right.

"After last night he really didn't think there was any hope," Emma explained.

"Where did he go?" Allyn asked somberly.

"Bogotá".

"Bogotá?" Hopelessness rang in Allyn's voice.

"He's taking a plane to Mexico City and going from there to Colombia. He leaves at nine." Emma glanced up at the clock. Eight-fifteen. "I doubt if you could make it, but—"

Allyn threw a "Thanks, all I can do is try" over her shoulder and ran across the grounds to the garage.

Even though the sun was out this morning, the air was cold. The van was reluctant to start and Allyn cursed herself for not having given it that tune-up she knew it needed before the cold weather hit. "Come on, baby," she coaxed. "I promise I'll have you winterized if you'll just start for me now."

As if in response, the engine started on the fifth try, and Allyn left an inch of tire rubber in the garage as she peeled out of it.

The highway was virtually empty on an early Sunday morning. Allyn raced down it, only half-looking for any sign of a police car that could pull her over for doing seventy instead of fifty-five. She made good time and her hopes lifted as she crossed over the valley highway.

She'd make it. She had to.

And then the motor began to cut out. The van chugged.

"Don't do this to me! Not now! Please..." She downshifted and eased into the right lane. "I'll get you the highest grade of oil, the best air filter, just please don't die."

It died anyway.

She coasted to the off ramp, yanked on the emergency brake and pounded the steering wheel three times—hard—before jumping out to look under the hood. She pushed up the sleeves on her navy blue turtleneck sweater with two fast swipes and set to work on the carburetor.

No luck. She tried everything she had ever done to the engine. Nothing worked. It was dead as a doornail and so were her hopes.

Eight thirty-five.

In twenty-five minutes Ian would get on a plane for Bogotá and fly out of her life. And she could have been at the airport in twenty.

She kicked the side of the van so hard she dented it.

She *had* to get to the airport. But how?

She could hitchhike.

Hitchhike?

Dear Lord. Hitchhiking was something foolish teenagers did when rebelliousness persuaded them to court danger. It wasn't something a thirty-three-year-old woman did. Not even when her car broke down.

But if she did...

Heedless of the grease on her hands, she thrust them into the pockets of her pale blue corduroy slacks. Hitchhiking was just plain crazy. It was offering yourself as the victim of rapists, robbers, murderers....

It was the only way she was going to get to Ian.

Reluctantly, Allyn took her left hand from her pocket, made a fist and flipped her thumb out into the wind.

Creeps beware, I have mace on my key ring.

Big deal.

As she walked, thumb out, she only half hoped someone would stop as she mentally searched for another course of action. How much would it cost to fly to Bogotá? Would her parents lend her the money? Could she find Ian once she arrived?

You've got it bad, Danner.

And then the worst possible scenario played itself out—a motorcycle passed, then stopped just ahead of her.

Allyn could feel the blood drain out of her face. Straddling the big metal monster, the driver pivoted toward her and motioned her to come and hop on. Hair down to the middle of his back, an unkempt beard and mustache, a red bandana tied around his forehead, a black leather jacket with studs all over it, black leather gloves with the fingers cut out and spikes on the knuckles....

How insulted would he be if she refused to take the ride her thumb had asked for in the first place? Other cars sped past. No one even looked her way. She could probably be murdered right there on the side of the road and not a soul would even slow down.

Again the man motioned.

Allyn pretended to have a stone in her shoe, taking it off and upturning it to give herself time to think.

The biker or Bogotá? What a choice!

At least the back of the black leather jacket didn't have the name of a gang emblazoned across it.

Think of Willie Nelson.

Wouldn't it be easier to jump from the back of a motorcycle than out of a car?

She put her shoe back on.

"That your van back there?" the biker said as she walked up.

"It's stalled," she said needlessly. "And I have to get to the airport in fifteen minutes."

"Climb on."

Trying to hide her hesitancy, Allyn swung her leg over the rear of the motorcycle. Once there, she didn't know what to do with her hands and feet.

"Put 'em up on the foot pegs there, lady, and hang on to me."

Touch him?

Only gingerly. Until he kicked the thing into gear, and she nearly did a backward somersault onto the highway. Then she held on for dear life.

The chill of autumn air bit into Allyn's face as the motorcycle raced in a loud drone. Her nose and ears began to hurt, and she wondered why anyone chose this mode of transportation. At least the van had a heater.

Would she be on time? She watched the road signs. Would the driver, around whose fleshy waist her arms were clasped, turn off on the airport exit? Or would he keep going?

Woman's body found in field....

How beat-up would a person get if she jumped off a thing like this traveling at a high speed?

But when the airport exit appeared the motorcycle turned onto it. Stapleton Airport came into view. A Continental Airlines jet took off to the north. A Lear jet came in from the west. And some of Allyn's trepidation about taking a ride from the motorcyclist turned to worry about Ian again.

Did I hurt you too much to still want me, Ian? Be resilient. Please be resilient. Please love me enough to understand.

In unconscious response to her own thoughts, Allyn tensed, and her grip of the driver's waist tightened reflexively. He glanced over his shoulder and smiled at her, one bushy, spiky eyebrow rising in a pleased question. She suddenly realized she was hugging the man hard and immediately let go of all but the lightest grip to keep herself from falling off as he took a corner sharply.

"What airline?" the man called back.

"Mexicana." Were planes delayed by flat tires? She wished one on this flight. Hurry....

The biker did what Allyn disapproved of most—he popped out of the lane and drove between two slower moving cars.

Motorcycle crushed between lanes....

The car drivers gave them dirty looks that Allyn met with a sheepish smile. But regardless of the methods, she was grateful when he pulled to a stop at the Mexicana entrance.

"Can I pay you?" she asked hurriedly, swinging off as if she'd been doing it all her life.

"Nah, glad to do it" was all he said around a grin that showed a wide gape between his two front teeth.

"Thanks, then," she said, and ran into the airport, vowing never to think another bad thing about a motorcycle driver again.

Ten minutes after nine.

Had it been Ian's plane that had just taken off overhead?

Allyn stopped at a television screen that listed the flights, her heartbeat drumming in her ears. Flight 306 had been delayed fifteen minutes. It didn't say if it was because of a flat tire, and she didn't care. Concourse A. Gate D. She ran.

Would he look at her with cold, contempt-filled eyes? Would he say what she would have said to Keith: No, I just don't want you anymore?

Mexicana's waiting area was crowded. A man at the ticket counter picked up a microphone and informed the passengers with small children that they could board. Allyn scanned the faces in a hurry. Ian wasn't there. More slowly, her gaze made a second trip, traveling the rows of people sitting, the groups standing at the windows watching the activities on the tarmac below, those boarding. Ian was definitely not among them. Even though her face and hands were still beet red from the cold, Allyn felt hot. Could he be in the men's room? She spun around in search but there wasn't one near. She had passed a bar not far down the corridor, but with the plane boarding, he wouldn't be there.

She didn't know what to do. Fear had created an image of the plane leaving before she arrived. It had shown her Ian rejecting her. It hadn't conjured up just not finding him. She tried the ticket counter.

"Could you tell me if Ian Reed is on this flight?"

A woman looked at her dubiously, but scanned a clipboard in front of her. "Yes, he is."

"Has he boarded?"

"Does he have a small child?"

"No," she said too impatiently. "I'm sorry. It's just that I have to find him. It's an emergency."

"He's flying first-class. Have you tried the VIP waiting room?" The woman pointed to the left, and Allyn hurried in that direction as the ticket agent called after her, "If he's not there come back and I'll page him."

But he was there, in a seat at the far end of a room that smelled of coffee and cigarettes.

For a moment Allyn was frozen in the doorway, watching him as he refolded the *Wall Street Journal* and put it into a leather carryon at his feet. He wore khaki pants and a pink cable-knit sweater, with just a band of a tan shirt collar showing above the crew neck. Even dressed casually he exuded power and dignity. A familiar flash of doubt shot through Allyn as she stood in postmotorcycle muss and watched a very put-together, sophisticated-looking woman smile at him when he looked up from his bag.

"Excuse me," said a man waiting for Allyn to move out of the doorway.

She stepped aside, and it was then that Ian's face turned to her. She hadn't realized his features were tense until he caught sight of her and she watched them ease slightly. His expression turned questioning, but he stayed where he was, not coming to her as she would have liked, not making it easier for her.

But she had come this far.

Allyn crossed the room. What should she say? she wondered as she sat gingerly on the edge of the chair next to his.

When she didn't speak, it was Ian who began in a tone that was unnervingly wry. "Come to say good-bye?"

"Not exactly," she hedged.

Over the speaker a voice announced boarding for all passengers.

"I . . ." But still she couldn't find the words to begin. *Open up. Tell him how you feel, why you came after him.* But suddenly the risk of rejection was greater than any she had ever consciously courted. And she was scared silly. She could say only "No, I didn't come to say goodbye."

Ian watched her intently. "Do you want to tell me why you did come, or shall I just get on that plane and wonder?"

Allyn looked at the floor, at the people filing out of the room, anywhere but at Ian. Her voice was quiet. "Could you take another flight?"

"I could," he said conversationally. "But I'm not sure I want to."

Her heart sank, and the color that cold air had painted on her face paled.

"If you've come to offer rhetoric about your independence I'd rather catch my plane. If you're here to give me what I want..."

That helped. She swallowed the lump in her throat. "Do you still want it?"

"Do you mean do I still want you?"

She could only nod her head.

For a long, agonizing moment, silence fell. Allyn could feel his eyes on her, but she couldn't bear to look at him. Then, finally, he answered his own question. "Yes, I do."

A good measure of tension drained out of her.

He put some back. "But only under the right conditions."

"Which are?"

Again the silence between them was filled by the disembodied voice from the speaker requesting that any passengers who had not boarded now do so.

Ian seemed in no hurry. "I've done a lot of talking, offering, showing good faith, telling you how I feel," he said dispassionately. "It's your turn."

"I still don't know what the right conditions are." She hedged again.

"Let's see if you can't meet them on your own."

"Okay," she burst out impatiently. "You were right about the fears from my past, about my protective isolation. But even I didn't understand it completely until this morning. I was beating you to the punch, as Sylvia said, dumping you before you could do it to me the way

Keith did. Not on purpose. It just sort of happened. I'm sorry.''

She thought his expression softened, saddened a little, but her words came out in a nervous rush as she shifted her gaze out the window to stare at the plane's tail. ''What Sylvia helped me to see was that feeling so repulsive that no one could really love me or stay with me was a remnant of damage that had more power than it should have had. I am not revolting or inadequate or anything else that makes me less than anyone else. Leaving me was an act of stupidity on Keith's part. It wasn't my fault, because of some major shortcoming of mine. So I love you and—'' the words had slipped out and surprised her. She stopped cold, not knowing what else to say.

''And if I had any brains I'd love you back and never leave you.''

That sounded about right but much too arrogant to say. Allyn merely shrugged.

Ian laughed then, a full, happy sound in the now empty room. ''That was the only condition you needed to fill.''

She looked at him then, questioningly.

''To tell me you loved me. Unless, of course, that doesn't mean you're going to marry me, in which case I'm still getting on that plane to Bogotá.''

As if on cue the voice from the speaker made the last call for passengers to board flight 306.

''I'm still going to expand Danner's Decadent Desserts and work like a fool,'' she warned.

He smiled, slow and steady. ''There was never a doubt in my mind. After the way I sold you to the

Markorts, if you don't make good on their investment, I'll be ruined myself.''

She had gone from not being able to look at him to not being able to get enough of the sight of him. Her tone was more serious. ''I do love you, Ian. More than I've ever loved anyone.''

''As much as it means to me to hear that, at this second it's just as important for me to know if you trust me not to hurt you the way you've been hurt before.''

''You mean do I feel safe with you?'' She pondered it with exaggerated solemnity. ''I guess there has to be some reason I risked my life to hitchhike on the back of a motorcycle driven by someone who looked like a mass murderer to get here. That must mean you make me feel pretty secure with life in general.''

''You're going to have to explain that one to me.''

''Another time.'' Allyn stood to look out the window as the plane taxied out to the runway. ''I think you've missed your flight, Reed.''

He came up from behind, wrapped his arms tightly around her and pulled her up close to him. ''And what about you, Danner?'' he murmured into her hair. ''Are you going to run out of here now to deliver desserts?''

She smiled seductively, her jubilant face reflected in the glass for him to see. ''Not a chance. I have the whole day off.''

''And I know just how to spend it.''

Within half an hour Ian had maneuvered her into a cab that took them to the row of hotels that lined Quebec Street, across from the airport, and registered them into a suite—with only one bedroom this time. By silent agreement they hastily undressed and fell into the king-size bed where they made love in an urgent need to reclaim each other.

When they were both sated and lay melded together in blissful fatigue, it was Ian who spoke, his lips against her temple. "Forever, love," he whispered.

"Forever love—just the kind I want," she teased him.

"I'm going to send your ex-husband a thank-you card. Otherwise he'll never know how grateful I am that he let you go. I love you, Allyn."

She laughed lightly. "When you send the card I think I'll have to sign it, too. Until now, I never knew how much of a favor he actually did for me." She craned her head back and kissed him, playfully tugging at first his lower lip and then his upper. "Do you think we'll ever see each other once you start traveling the world making mergers and I become a dessert mogul?"

"I expect a little compromising—you know, a good dose of delegating authority and responsibilities, once Danner's Decadent Desserts is off the ground. I have every intention of showing you the most beautiful sights the world has to offer, of making love to you in every one of them."

She laughed, for the first time looking forward to the idea of hiring people to take over for her. "We're going to make love on top of the Eiffel Tower? In the Leaning Tower of Pisa? Behind Big Ben? You didn't tell me you were kinky."

"In a field of heather in Wales. In a Swiss chalet in the Alps. In a garret in Paris. In the back of the new van I'm going to buy you as a wedding present. On the floor in front of the ovens while the tortes bake. Here. Now."

"I think you're a sex maniac," she said with lascivious delight.

"By all means, let me confirm it." He dipped down to trace the hollow of her throat with his tongue. Allyn halfheartedly pushed him away.

"I don't know about that. It just occurred to me that we aren't practicing birth control."

His grin was so broad it nearly went ear to ear. "It occurred to me right from the start."

"Then there was method to this madness."

"If madness this be—" he began a rain of kisses "—let's have lots and lots of it."

"You'd better marry me quick," she moaned as his mouth reached the crest of her breast and his tongue made sweet torment there.

"Gladly. This will only take about an hour, and then we'll get right to it."

It took two hours.

And then they did indeed get right to it.

* * * * *

WHEN OPPOSITES ATTRACT

Roberta Malcolm had spent her life on the Mescalero ranch. Then Hollywood—and Jed Pulaski—came to Mescalero, and suddenly everything changed.

Jed Pulaski had never met anyone like Rob Malcolm. Her forthright manner hid a woman who was beautiful, vibrant—and completely fascinating. But Jed knew their lives were as far apart as night from day, and only an all-consuming love could bring them together, forever, in the glory of dawn.

Look for Jed and Roberta's story in *That Malcolm Girl*, IM #253, Book Two of Parris Afton Bonds's Mescalero Trilogy, available next month only from Silhouette Intimate Moments. Then watch for Book Three, *That Mescalero Man* (December 1988), to complete the trilogy.

Silhouette Intimate Moments

SET SAIL FOR THE SOUTH SEAS
with
BESTSELLING AUTHOR
EMILIE RICHARDS

This month Silhouette Intimate Moments begins a very special miniseries by a very special author. *Tales of the Pacific*, by Emilie Richards, will take you to Hawaii, New Zealand and Australia and introduce you to a group of men and women you will never forget.

In Book One, FROM GLOWING EMBERS, share laughter and tears with Julianna Mason and Gray Sheridan as they overcome the pain of the past and rekindle the love that had brought them together in marriage ten years ago and now, amidst the destructive force of a tropical storm, drives them once more into an embrace without end.

FROM GLOWING EMBERS (Intimate Moments #249) is available now. And in coming months look for the rest of the series: SMOKESCREEN (November 1988), RAINBOW FIRE (February 1989) and OUT OF THE ASHES (May 1989). They're all coming your way—only in Silhouette Intimate Moments.

IM249-R

ATTRACTIVE, SPACE SAVING BOOK RACK

Display your most prized novels on this handsome and sturdy book rack. The hand-rubbed walnut finish will blend into your library decor with quiet elegance, providing a practical organizer for your favorite hard-or soft-covered books.

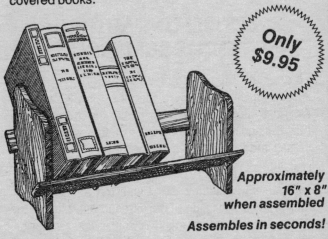

Only $9.95

Approximately 16" x 8" when assembled

Assembles in seconds!

To order, rush your name, address and zip code, along with a check or money order for $10.70* ($9.95 plus 75¢ postage and handling) payable to *Silhouette Books.*

Silhouette Books
Book Rack Offer
901 Fuhrmann Blvd.
P.O. Box 1396
Buffalo, NY 14269-1396

Offer not available in Canada.

*New York and Iowa residents add appropriate sales tax.

BKR-2A